LUCILLE'S VALENTINE

Vampires of London Book 3

LORELEI MOONE

CONTENTS

PROLOGUE

Ever since Lucille had hauled the criminal known as Marek before the Council, she could not wait for the trial to begin. She had so many questions and very few answers. Her curiosity was what made her such a driven investigator.

Marek was a Soul Eater; that much was clear. But how had he become so powerful? How old was he? How long had he been killing humans indiscriminately without appearing on her radar?

Obviously, he had only just started his reign of terror in London a few weeks ago, when a human had been found on the brink of death by one of their own. The vampire Michael had turned the unfortunate female, and Lucille had worked together with the unlikely pair to track down Marek and his henchmen.

It had been a triumphant victory for her, and earned her much praise from Julius, Lucille's maker and leader of the Council.

Tonight was finally going to be the night. The trial of Marek and his associates would begin.

He stood accused of reckless conduct that risked the exposure of the vampire race to humanity as well as attempted murder of a fellow vampire. Julius had wanted to add on more charges, but decided against it on Lucille's advice. They had caught him on the gravest crime possible. The Council took the safety of their kind extremely seriously. And randomly draining humans and leaving them for all the world to find was the most callous display of overt vampirism the city had seen in over a century. The only way the Council could have come down any harder on Marek would have been if he'd videotaped himself drinking his victim's blood and posted it on the Internet.

So it wasn't the outcome of the trial that Lucille was interested in; the case was clear and the punishment obvious; Marek would be sentenced to death, and depending on whether they were complicit or only following orders, so would his two associates. Lucille was more interested in any possible justifications Marek would give during the process. Any information at all that would shine a light on his motivations and history.

Lucille would be lying to herself if she didn't admit that Marek's immense power had intrigued and even impressed her a bit. He had been a formidable adversary.

Additionally, there was something about the vehemence with which Julius sought to punish Marek that had set off her investigative instincts. There was something more to their relationship than the Council leader had led on.

"Are you ready, my child?" Julius interrupted her thoughts.

"Yes, of course." Lucille looked up and nodded at her

maker.

The most powerful vampire in the world, as Julius liked to refer to himself at times. It was true in a political sense. His claim for the Council leadership had gone unchallenged for centuries. Though Marek had shown powers that outshone Julius manifold. Was that his reason for disliking the Soul Eater so much?

He returned her nod and beckoned her to come closer.

"It'll all be over soon. Before long, Marek will no longer be able to threaten our way of life."

Lucille scrutinized the smug grin on Julius' face. He was definitely hiding something.

"Have you come across him before?" she asked.

Julius glanced at her, his face suddenly serious again. "We've known of the Soul Eaters that live outside the Council's realm of influence for centuries. You know this. Never before have they ventured into London, though."

None who were this evolved, no. Though Lucille had dealt with plenty of killers before.

That hadn't answered her question, but Lucille decided not to pry. Due to their history, Julius had a soft spot for her, but it would be unwise to exploit their relationship just to get answers out of him. Perhaps she was just being nosy. What business was it of hers whether or not Julius knew the Soul Eater from another time?

"I will call in the elders," Lucille said. "Once everyone is here we can begin."

Julius shot her a quick smile and rubbed his hands

together. "Very good, my child."

Lucille left the main hall and rounded up the other six members of the Council. Although she was already four centuries old, the elders, as the term suggested, were all much more senior. At least a millennium old, each one of them. Together, they represented the far corners of the world, both ancient and modern. As the six venerable vampires entered the great hall, Lucille found herself captivated by their movements. Some seemed to levitate rather than walk, but each demonstrated a smoothness and elegance of movement that Lucille herself could not replicate if she wanted to.

Vampires, those that had the capacity to outlast the age they were born in, got better and more impressive with age.

They sat on the six chairs arranged in a semi-circle around Julius' throne. Three to his left and three to his right. There were further chairs inside the main hall facing the throne for any other vampires who wished to observe the trial. The center of the hall had been kept free for the accused.

Lucille signaled at Dominic and Cameron, the two guards stationed beside the large entrance doors, to let the audience in.

Whispers and footsteps echoed against the tall ceiling of the cathedral as about three dozen vampires shuffled inside and found their seats. Then, Julius raised his right hand and the crowd became silent.

"We are gathered here for the trial of Marek the Soul Eater and his two progenies, who shall remain unnamed," Julius spoke in a firm voice.

A whisper traveled across the audience once again.

"So it's true."

"A Soul Eater!"

"I can't believe it!"

Lucille rolled her eyes. The sort of vampires who frequented Council trials were not her usual choice of company. Then again, not many people were.

Julius cleared his throat and silence prevailed once more. "Bring in the prisoners!"

Lucille watched as the double doors swung open and two more Council guards rolled in a cage on wheels that gleamed under the chandelier in the center of the hall. The Silver Vault, as it was known, was only used during trials of the most notorious, dangerous criminals. Obviously, Marek posed a flight risk; his powers were greater than those of anyone in this room. Perhaps he was even stronger than Julius himself.

Marek's two associates were led in wearing cuffs right behind the cage.

The audience was deadly silent as the three accused were positioned in the empty space between the council members and the rest of the crowd.

Julius cleared his throat again and got up from his throne.

"Marek. You know why you are here. You are to stand

trial—"

Marek shook his head. "Julius, please refer to me by my full title."

Lucille frowned. Julius and Marek did seem awfully familiar, the way they spoke to one another.

Julius' eyes narrowed. "Very well. Marek, son of Lilith. You are on trial for—"

Lilith. Only the most ancient of vampires held the title son or daughter of Lilith. Julius held this title himself. That meant Marek was an ancient? A contender for a seat on the Council?

"The rest also, if you don't mind. I've worked too hard these past millennia for my achievements to go unnoticed."

Lucille found that she was holding her breath. Marek had guts to interrupt Julius twice in front of an entire room full of his subjects. Then again, he probably knew as well as any of them that his life would soon be over, so he had nothing much to lose.

"Son of Lilith, Master of a Thousand Souls." Julius folded his arms and stared darkly at Marek. How long would his patience last?

"Thank you." Marek grinned, showing off a row of razor sharp white teeth.

During the brief contact Lucille had had with Marek, he had not struck her as one of those vampires who grew weary of immortality and longed for it all to end. Yet here he was, taunting Julius and grinning like a madman on what could very well be his last day walking this earth. It wasn't just unusual, it was unnerving.

Julius ignored Marek's remark and started listing his offenses, during which Marek seemed to grow even more cheerful. He was obviously proud of everything he'd done.

Lucille found herself tuning out Julius' monotone voice. It was all stuff she'd heard before. Killing humans, leaving their bodies, risking their exposure, blah, blah.

Instead of listening to him rehashing the same old accusations, she took the time to really observe Marek. His strange appearance had fascinated her from the moment she'd first laid eyes on him.

Vampires didn't age normally, but in the case of Marek, he seemed marked by every century he'd lived through. The casual observer might mistake his transparent skin, his slender body, and papery voice for signs of frailty. Lucille knew otherwise. It had taken a dozen guards to subdue Marek and restrain him for transport back to the Council prison.

The two younger Soul Eaters who stood toward his left now looked much more powerful, but actually did not even possess half of Marek's strength. Lucille found it difficult to control her curiosity. She knew of vampires who'd killed humans; she had locked up many of them over the years. But these three were different. They didn't just kill, they had figured out a way of absorbing a victim's essence—their strength and life-force. Not just their blood.

Was it magic?

She could not make sense of it on her own, and seeing as Julius seemed in no mood to share whatever information or previous knowledge of Marek he had… She would talk to Alexander about it as soon as the trial was over. Perhaps her brother and his vast library of old books could shed some light.

Lucille rested her gaze on the younger Soul Eater who stood nearest to the Silver Vault. He seemed unafraid, like his maker, smiling subtly and staring at nothing in particular, until suddenly he looked up right into Lucille's eyes.

A shiver travelled down her spine, but she did not let it show.

If you want to live, you'll stand down.

So he was a telepath, and a rather talented one too, if he could communicate with her halfway across the large hall.

Lucille did not take kindly to threats. Her hand instinctively reached for the dagger she kept in a sheath attached to her belt. She snapped open the clasp that held the blade in place and tightened her fingers around the grip.

She looked back at Marek, who had started to laugh. A quick glance at Julius revealed that he was starting to lose his cool. He spoke faster now, lecturing the three accused on the codes of conduct the Council lived by and promoted. His eyes were wild, his expression even tenser than before.

Lucille looked back at Marek, who had now reached for the bars on his cage, tightening his long, bony fingers around them. The scent of burning flesh filled the air as his skin reacted to the metal. An ordinary vampire would not be able to bear it, but Marek showed no sign of being in pain. Instead of letting go, he held on tighter, tugging at it until the bars started to give way.

Lucille jumped forward, her dagger drawn, and was instantly joined by the guards who had been positioned at the doors. The crowd gasped in horror as Marek's form became blurred, his body twisting and whirling around so fast that even Lucille's perfect vision could no longer focus on him. His laughter echoed through the Council chamber, growing louder and louder until it became deafening.

She reached the cage, but Marek was no longer inside. Instead, he seemed to be levitating far above the ground, still turning at lightning speed, like a whirlwind. Now what? She didn't have his talents or his powers; she could do nothing but watch.

Lucille turned and saw that Julius was frozen in place in front of his throne, his fist raised in the air in protest, lips opening and closing, without any sound coming out.

She had never seen him stumped like this.

At that moment, the stained glass of the large rosette shaped window above Julius' throne shattered as Marek's floating form surged against it and broke through. He was gone within the blink of an eye.

"Go after him," Julius hissed, before repeating himself much louder and forcefully. "Go after him at once!"

Lucille turned and found that Julius had moved from his throne. He now stood just a few feet away from her near the Silver Vault, with Marek's two followers slumped in pools of blood at his feet. After the initial shock of Marek's grand display, Julius had recovered and taken swift action and punished them with death. Their still twitching hearts lay on the ground beside their lifeless bodies.

"Yes, master," Lucille mumbled. It had been extremely difficult capturing Marek the first time around. This time, she would need a miracle.

CHAPTER ONE

Valentino Conti dealt in death.

He knew it, and those unfortunate creatures he was after found out soon enough.

But for the past month and a half, he had been tracking something else, something much more depraved than everything he'd already seen in his illustrious career. Something that managed to send shivers down even his spine.

That was why he was here tonight, on this cold, dark January night. He navigated the corridors deep inside Waterloo train station leading to the video surveillance control room, which was normally off limits to outsiders. It was through sheer tenacity, as well as a heavy dose of Mediterranean charm and a significant sum of money, that he had found a way in with one of the camera operators.

He waited at the agreed spot and checked his watch. The woman better be on time. If this lead panned out, it would be by far his most important achievement yet.

Valentino's hunt had started, like so many other quests, with a short anonymous message on an online forum about the supernatural. To the casual observer, these websites looked like the paranoid ravings of horror movie obsessed teenagers, but Valentino and those in his line of work knew better.

Someone had spotted a creature in London that was so bizarre the mere description of it had inspired Valentino to get on a plane and investigate it himself.

Years spent as a hunter had taught him not to be too presumptuous. Nightwalkers—or vampires, as they were known in the common tongue—came in all manner of forms. Some seemed almost normal—human, like himself. Others were obviously otherworldly.

Either way, the description he read had reminded him of old stories his grandfather had told him when he was just a little boy, of a Nightwalker so powerful and evil, he even inspired terror in his peers.

Upon arriving in London, he had heard of a string of deaths attributed to a new serial killer. It hadn't been too difficult to come by autopsy photos of the victims; such items had a way of leaking to the press or even private collectors.

Despite how the authorities and the media had spun it, Valentino was certain the deaths were the result of vampire activity. But since the crime scenes had not been discovered yet, he couldn't prove any of his suspicions.

Footsteps approached, and soon, the skittish looking woman in uniform came into view. She checked that she wasn't being followed, then nodded at Valentino to join her in one of the corridors leading off to the right. It was obvious from her entire demeanor that she had never done anything like this before. She was scared.

"There's no cameras in here," she whispered.

"You've got the footage?" he asked.

She glanced over her shoulder again, then retrieved a folded printout from her pocket. "They've installed some new security features. I couldn't risk it with the pen drive. But I did manage to print off a still," she said, thrusting the paper into Valentino's hand.

It was disappointing not to get the original video, but a still was better than nothing. He nodded at her and handed her a sealed envelope.

"It's all there," he said.

"Thanks. I really must be off now." She turned on her heel, ready to leave, then paused. "The image, it's a little blurry, but it's the best I could find. Some kind of camera glitch, perhaps. The man you're after, he looks a bit distorted. Hopefully it's good enough."

It was too late to change his mind. He'd already handed her the rest of the payment, and he was a man of his word. Whatever was on that printout, it would have to do.

"No problem, darling. If you find anything else, do get in touch." He shot her a quick smile.

The woman gave him a brief nod, then made a quick exit. It was unlikely he'd hear from her again.

Valentino waited until she was out of sight before unfolding the piece of paper she'd given him. The sight of it took his breath away.

So this was who—or rather, what—he was hunting.

The figure was humanoid in form, if you ignored the spindly arms and legs. Its robes seemed to cling to it in a strange fashion as well, almost giving the appearance of black clouds or shadows. If you looked carefully, it seemed to be floating; its feet didn't appear to touch the ground.

Of course his insider had felt it was some kind of optical illusion, a malfunction in the camera equipment that had made the footage look so creepy. People outside his circles often preferred to remain in denial; he'd learned that the hard way a long time ago.

She had no idea what he was hunting and that was just as well.

Valentino knew better than to presume the same, though. The anonymous tipster whose forum post had brought him to London had been correct; this was a very peculiar creature indeed. And the image he saw in front of him bore an uncanny resemblance to the sketches his grandfather had shown him when he was just a boy. At the time he'd thought the old man was exaggerating; now he knew better.

How many monsters this vile could possibly walk the earth unnoticed? Valentino was certain it could not be a coincidence. It *had* to be the same one.

Valentino instinctively grabbed for the silver chain around his neck. The pendant hanging from it was the medal of St. Benedict, which had been in his family pretty much forever. He wasn't particularly religious, or even superstitious, so he wore the medal to remind him of his family's legacy rather than for its supposed powers for warding off evil spirits.

He would complete this mission for his late grandfather.

He studied the blurry surveillance photograph in front of him again.

This right here demonstrated the difference between hunting a creature in London, versus any other city he'd traveled to in the past: there were cameras everywhere. Of course, those people manning the cameras were a lot stricter about rules and regulations, but at the right price, one could procure anything.

His wallet was lighter tonight, but the price had been worth it.

A month of aimless canvassing had made him precious little progress, until tonight. In fact, he'd been close to giving up before the woman who worked in the control room had agreed to help. Now, Valentino felt revitalized.

He slipped the photograph into the inner pocket of his coat and zipped up tight. It was cold out there and he had a long night ahead of him. Tonight, he would start with the area around that particular surveillance camera. The time stamp on the image placed the creature in a back alley near Waterloo five whole nights ago.

Who knew, perhaps it had left some clues behind.

So that was his first destination. He made his way through the large station and exited.

As he progressed through the dark, wet streets, he felt the burden of this quest weigh heavily on him. His grandfather had not succeeded in catching this creature when he'd first come across it during the First World War. It had escaped and terrorized many a city and village since, and the resulting guilt had been difficult for him to live with.

Valentino was determined to succeed. If not for himself, then to honor his grandfather's memory. As it was, since the death of his father two years ago, Valentino was the last of the Conti clan still standing. A lot rested on him. Where even just a century ago, there had been multiple prominent hunter families in Italy alone, the Contis had been the last to endure. The modern world seemed to not have much room for his kind.

Meanwhile, the other side, the Nightwalker side, seemed to flourish in some parts. There had been a resurgence in vampire activity in Eastern Europe, even though the authorities had often explained any suspicious events away as cult activity. It was as though the Nightwalkers had become bolder and bolder over time. Perhaps they thought they were invincible, because there were not many able or willing to stop them.

He had to do his part to make a difference.

It was these and many more similar thoughts that occupied him as he reached the service lane beside the station where the creature had been captured on camera.

Valentino opened the leather messenger bag he always carried with him and retrieved a bottle of Luminol. Where there was a vampire, there was bound to be trace evidence of blood. He took a look around and identified a couple of dark corners ideal for the creature to attack and drain someone. One in particular, a grouping of garbage bins underneath a broken streetlights, seemed most likely. He sprayed the area surrounding the bins and inspected it for any fluorescent stains. Sure enough, there was some blood present, though not a lot. Just a fine spray pattern on the side of one of the containers. This was the kind of evidence one might find where a vampire had fed; puncturing a man's jugular to feed could result in a bit of spill-over.

But considering the area, the blood in itself was hardly definitive; the blood stains could have been the result of a human altercation, such as someone being struck hard enough to rupture skin. A big city like London had its ugly parts even without any supernatural influences.

Valentino put the spray away and took out a specially modified ultraviolet torch. Human saliva and other bodily fluids lit up under so-called black light, but their luminescence was dull compared to traces of vampire saliva.

Besides the blood splatter Valentino had just identified, there was a smear of something that glowed bright purple under his UV light. That was it. Conclusive evidence.

He took a sample, which he carefully sealed in a plastic pouch. One for the collection. Sometimes he wondered if he was wasting his time collecting samples and cataloging them in detail. He had prepared a file on each Nightwalker he had ever hunted; who knew, maybe one day all this stuff would come in handy.

Once he had labeled the sample and put it away, he took out a small, leather bound notebook and started to write. *Feeding site, alley near Waterloo station, date of attack: 3rd Jan.*

Where to next? Valentino looked around and spied an unassuming pub at the end of the road. Perhaps someone there remembered seeing something suspicious on that night, five days ago. Any establishment in a location like this would serve mostly travelers passing through. Still, the staff might have something to share.

Of course, he would be careful and only ask innocuous questions. The last time he had tried to be candid with someone who wasn't part of his world had backfired painfully.

Valentino was on his own. He could not count on anyone to help him defeat this monster.

He put the notebook away, securely buckled up the front of the bag, and resolutely marched in the direction of the lit up sign. As glamorous as it had seemed to him when he was younger, being a vampire hunter was mostly legwork and traditional detective work, only without the benefit of holding an official badge.

CHAPTER TWO

Lucille had followed the stranger from the alley, which still stank of the Soul Eater Marek, into a down-market pub at the end of the road. She had watched from a quiet, dark corner while he had spoken to the cranky bartender, who seemed unwilling to answer any of the questions with more than two syllables, and the young woman who worked the tap. It was obvious from the increasingly strained and tense body language of everyone involved that the stranger had not been able to get the information he was after.

Who was he?

His accent was unmistakably Italian, even if his English was very close to perfect. So perhaps he wasn't from here. In a cosmopolitan city such as London, that did not narrow things down.

Lucille had watched him earlier out on the road as he had scraped off some sort of substance from the side of a garbage container and put it in a bag. Now, realizing that the staff was no longer open to conversing with him, he sat down at an empty table with a pint and started scribbling away in that little notebook of his.

She would have to do a walk-by and read his notes over his shoulder at some point. It could, of course, be a coincidence that during the same week as Marek's daring escape from the Council chambers, some stranger had come along and started nosing around the exact place Lucille had come to investigate. If only Lucille believed in coincidences.

No, this man, with his strange equipment and affinity for sniffing out dark blood-stained corners, was definitely after the same thing as she was. He smelled human, so he wasn't back-up sent in by one of the other Council elders. That left only one possibility: he was a hunter.

Lucille had heard of vampire hunters active mostly in Eastern Europe, where she presumed Marek had traveled in from last month. They hardly ever came to London; why would they? The Council, and Lucille as their Enforcer, worked hard to keep vampire activity under wraps here.

But now, it seemed Marek's presence had attracted at least one of them.

The Council generally forbade the killing of humans, but if he got in her way, she might not have any other choice.

Lucille continued to watch as the man put down his pen and stared at the bar. If she wanted to sneak a peek at his notes, she had to hurry before he put them away.

She got up, empty glass in hand, and walked slowly and deliberately through the few tables that separated her dark corner from the vampire hunter's position. It took barely a second for her to read the page of notes. Funnily, they were in English, not Italian, as she would have expected, considering his accent. This truly was the age of globalization.

There wasn't a lot in there that Lucille didn't already know. He'd found a feeding site, obviously; that was why he had taken a sample. But the thing that surprised her was that the man had written down the date on which he thought Marek had been there. How could he possibly know that? *She* hadn't known that.

All she had been able to do was narrow down the time of the attack to 3-6 days ago. That was what her nose had told her, anyway, based on the deterioration of the blood stains Marek had left behind. Her estimation was as accurate as a human's might be, trying to decide the age of stale milk left out in warm weather. What methods did this hunter use that she was as yet unaware of?

She caught herself staring at the man's back and was forced back into action when she heard his heartbeat speed up just a little. He had sensed her presence.

Just as he turned his head to see who was looking at him, she had passed him by and reached the bar.

"Another, please." Lucille pointed at her empty glass, then at the bottle of her choice that stood on the shelf opposite her.

She wasn't much of a drinker, unlike her brother Alexander, who enjoyed his glass of brandy every night as though it was a sacred ritual. She didn't even like the taste of most drinks, certainly not those many women in this age seemed to favor. Everything was too sweet, too sickly.

The bartender glanced at her with a hint of bemusement in his eye as he poured her another Laphroaig single malt. Obviously, he thought it was an unusual choice for someone who looked like her. Then again, he had no way of knowing he was serving a nearly four-hundred year old vampire instead of the twenty-three year old young woman whose body she occupied.

She put the money on the bar without saying a word and was about to turn when she spied movement in a reflection on the bottles behind the bar.

"I'll have whatever she's having," the hunter said in his smooth Italian accent.

Lucille had learned how to blend into human society a long time ago. There was no way for him to know who—or what—she really was. She was just an attractive woman drinking alone in a dodgy bar near Waterloo. And despite his unusual and lethal calling, he was still a man. Her best option would be to play along.

"Suit yourself, but it's an acquired taste," she said, smiling subtly.

He was a fine specimen, this hunter. A chiseled jaw, full, sensual lips, and sun-kissed skin. She might have had a taste, if he was just a regular guy and not her sworn enemy.

But when she looked up into his eyes, something she saw in them tugged at her, constricting her chest and making her take a step back. *It can't be. It's been centuries.*

"It's best not to make assumptions about a man's taste," he said, letting his gaze rest on her lips.

Seriously. This guy was hunting the most dangerous vampire Lucille had ever come across in her four-hundred years of walking this earth and he thought it wise to flirt with her right now? They were on opposing sides, but she was outraged all the same. Did he not take his work seriously at all?

Lucille avoided eye contact and shrugged. "That goes for women's tastes too."

The bartender poured the hunter's drink but kept quiet otherwise. His disapproval of the hunter was obvious, though; he was probably still irritated by his nosy interrogation earlier.

"Salute! How do you say…" He raised his glass in Lucille's direction.

Again, best to just play the part. "Cheers!" she said.

"Ah yes, cheers."

They both took a sip, which Lucille savored. Peaty. Just like it said on the label.

"Wow, this sure is something else," the hunter remarked. He sniffed the glass, then swirled the remaining dark amber liquid around in it.

"Told you." Lucille straightened herself. What was she doing? The look in his eyes made her feel uncomfortable, almost threatened. Perhaps she should let him know she wasn't interested and get on with her work.

"I like it, though." The hunter smiled and stuck out his right hand. "Valentino Conti. Pleasure to meet you."

His name rang a bell, like she'd heard it before. Lucille

reluctantly accepted his greeting. His skin burned against hers almost painfully. So warm. So alive. It occurred to her that in trying to hunt down Marek, it had been a while since she'd last fed.

"Lucille Amboise. I really should be off, though," she said.

Valentino raised an eyebrow. "But you've only just bought a drink. And your hand was so cold I'd worry about you freezing to death out there."

Lucille stared down at her glass. An excellent point about the drink. She should just hypnotize him. Get it over with. But what if he had some kind of technology to counter it? She would give herself away.

"You're absolutely right, of course. I suppose I'm just nervous," she said. It was only a half-lie. There was something about him that had made her uneasy, and it hadn't been the fact that he would try to kill her if he knew what she was. It was those eyes, those warm, infuriatingly friendly eyes that sought to bore a hole in her soul.

The eyes that seemed to belong to someone who died a very long time ago.

"Aw, I did not mean to make you nervous. Why don't we have a seat and chat," he suggested with a smile.

Lucille looked at the table he was gesturing at, the one he'd sat at while she was spying on him, and shrugged. "I suppose I can stay a little while longer."

Perhaps if she got him talking, she could figure out more about what he was doing here and what else he had found out. She wasn't the sort to lose her nerve easily. How hard could it be to practice her poker face for little while longer and see what she could learn?

"Are you a regular here?" Valentino asked as he pushed her chair in for her.

Lucille looked up and cocked her head to the side. "Are you asking me if I 'come here often?'" she teased.

The man laughed. "I see, that came out wrong. The truth is I'm looking for a man who might have been in the area a few days ago."

Lucille pressed her lips together. He had a strange technique. Going from flirting with her to questioning her about Marek in just a short exchange.

"On the third, to be precise."

"Friend of yours? The man you're looking for, I mean." Now it was her turn to start interrogating.

Valentino smiled and shook his head. "Not exactly."

"Well I'm just not entirely sure why I should help you. I know nothing about your motivations. What if you wish to harm this man?" Lucille argued and took another sip.

The hunter observed her, then followed her example, putting his glass down on the wooden table when he was done.

"Let me ask you something: Do you believe in destiny? That perhaps we were meant to meet here tonight because you could help me find what I'm looking for?"

Lucille frowned. She couldn't make out if he was still prying for information or flirting again. Very strange technique indeed. ·

"Not everything can be explained by science," she responded.

Valentino nodded. "Indeed. Well, perhaps not yet. Anyway, this man I'm looking for is dangerous. I'm just trying to keep people from harm."

Okay, so it was still an interrogation.

"You're trying to save the world, is that it?" she said.

He laughed again. Lucille folded her arms. She hadn't even tried to be funny. Jokes were not her forte.

"I suppose you could put it that way. You don't believe me, do you?"

Lucille shrugged. "Whatever helps you sleep at night."

Valentino pulled out the leather notebook from his messenger bag and placed it on the table in front of them. Then he flipped to a different page than Lucille had seen when she read over his shoulder earlier.

"I believe a murder has been committed just down the street from here. And the man I'm looking for did it."

He held up the book, showing her a pencil sketch of a group of garbage bins, the ones where he'd taken his samples earlier. Off to the side of the bins stood two dark figures; one had the other by the throat. Blood splatters were scribbled on in red ink.

"How do you know this?" Lucille asked. "Are you with the police?"

Valentino shook his head. "The evidence is right there for anyone to find."

Lucille picked up her glass and emptied it. "Well, why don't you show me?"

The hunter stared at her face while she did her best not to look into his eyes again. "Has anyone ever told you you're quite unusual? One moment you want to leave, the next you want to go look around a dark alley for clues with me?"

"I read a lot of detective novels. Perhaps I want to see a real one in action," she said.

He smiled again and nodded. "Why not. But on one condition."

"What's that?" Lucille asked.

"You let me buy you another drink when we're done. It really is cold outside."

CHAPTER THREE

Valentino stole a glance at Lucille as they left the pub together. What a peculiar young woman. Everything about her, from the way she carried herself to her choice of Scotch signaled that she was an old soul. The fact that she had joined him out here meant that apparently she was fearless as well.

Was she part of the same underground he belonged to? The online message boards, the discussion groups that met virtually to discuss any supernatural activity they had come across. It had been one of those anonymous reports of vampirism that had brought him to London in the first place. Was she active in those circles? Or was her presence here a coincidence?

Her catlike movements as she walked alongside him toward the feeding site suggested she was strong and well trained. She definitely knew how to fight.

He wouldn't be surprised if she had some hidden weapons somewhere underneath her long coat. He had some too, after all.

When they reached the bin he had inspected on his own earlier, he pulled out the bottle of Luminol again and sprayed the area where he knew the blood to be.

She leaned in closer and followed the direction of the spray pattern with her index finger.

"Interesting."

Valentino smiled. "As I said, the evidence is right here."

Lucille stood back and stared at the ground surrounding the area. "It wasn't much of a struggle, so perhaps the victim came here willingly."

Valentino raised an eyebrow. "How do you know this?"

Lucille pointed at a very faint muddy footprint which the winter rains had done their best to erase. "If two men had fought here, they would have knocked over some of these bags of rubbish. They would have left smudged prints and scuff marks from their shoes. I don't see any of that here."

She turned to face him, her eyes narrow and darting back and forth between him and their surroundings. "Do you think the murderer might have arrived here by train? Or is he a local?"

"I think he is not the sort of man who could travel by train without drawing too much attention to himself. He is the sort who stays in the shadows."

Lucille nodded, as though she understood him perfectly, even those things he'd left unsaid. She really was peculiar, unlike any woman he'd met before.

Could he risk it?

It had been a long time since he'd ever told an outsider about his calling, and that had backfired spectacularly. Suddenly years of history didn't matter anymore, and the woman he'd opened up to because he wanted to spend his life with her had simply left.

But this right here was different; there was no history. What did he have to lose?

"There are more things between heaven and earth than most people choose to see or believe…"

Lucille folded her arms as she focused on him. He had her full attention.

"This murderer is not strictly a *man*," Valentino added.

"Why. Is it a woman?" she asked, cocking her head to the side.

The peculiar glint in her eye told him that he was on the right track. She was testing him; Valentino would bet his life on it.

"He's a Nightwalker. A vampire."

Lucille pursed her lips and glanced at the bin with the blood evidence on it, then back at him. The corner of her mouth twitched in amusement; it was so subtle he would have missed it if he wasn't paying attention.

"You're a hunter," she remarked, as though it was the most natural thing in the world.

He nodded. She knew the terminology. Unless she was the best actress he'd ever come across, nothing he'd told her so far had shocked her in any way.

"You have unusual methods. More like a forensic investigator than a hunter," she added.

He nodded again. "And your methods? Old school. More like a tracker."

Lucille smiled briefly. "I favor a more intuitive approach."

"Have you been at this long?" he asked. He was thirty-four, not old by any stretch of the imagination, but Lucille looked about ten years younger—exceptionally young for someone in their line of work. Perhaps it was a family affair for her, just like it had been for him.

"My entire life," she said.

Fine, so she wanted to keep things vague. He didn't mind. Their line of work was lonely and unappreciated for the most part. To run into another hunter was its own reward. He didn't need anything more than that for now.

"How about you make good on that promise then?" she said. "Of buying me another drink."

Valentino grinned. If she didn't look so serious he might have thought she was flirting with him.

They walked back together, and he again marveled at her smooth, deliberate movements, the strong spring in her step. It was a lonely existence; living on the fringes of society, hunting creatures that most people only acknowledged in their nightmares.

The times had changed since his parents and grandparents had been around. Mainstream society no longer believed in the supernatural, as he had so painfully found out in the past. Continuing in their footsteps had earned him a solitary life. It would be a nice change of pace to combine forces with a like-minded soul.

Plus, Lucille was an exceptionally beautiful woman. He would be lying to himself if he thought that she hadn't affected him on some deeper level. But he'd been at this too long to simply take other people at face value. He still needed to find out if he could trust Lucille.

"Right. Let's get that drink then," he said.

———•◆•———

The conversation between them had flowed more freely from the second round on.

Now that Valentino was back at the guest house which had been his home for the past few weeks, he went through the events of the evening again in his head.

As he lay down on the bed, closing his eyes for a moment, he felt his body grow heavy. If he wasn't careful, sleep would claim him before he had the chance to finish analyzing his encounter with Lucille. He wasn't a big drinker, but in her company, he had indulged a little. The effects were only starting to wear off now, hours later.

Had he let his guard down too much?

She had been vague about her background, about how she'd found her start in hunting Nightwalkers. Instead, she'd mainly been a very good and supportive listener. And perhaps he'd ended up sharing more information with her than he should have.

It had been hard not to. Everything about her seemed especially designed to invite him in, to make him feel comfortable being his true self. Even the fact that on the surface, she seemed curt and difficult to impress. The challenge of getting closer to her had been irresistible.

The only things she'd shared were the odd hint or

remark suggesting she knew more about this vampire than she had initially let on. She'd spoken about how this monster was different from other vampires. More powerful. More devious. Above all, more dangerous.

Valentino already knew all that, but it was interesting to hear her say it. And it sparked the question: what made this vampire so fundamentally different? Was it age or something else? He was determined to get to the bottom of it, and despite some lingering reservations about his hunting partner, Valentino was certain she was the key to finding out.

They would hunt this monster together, and in the process, he hoped to find out everything there was to know about Lucille too.

———◆———

She stepped out of the fog and offered him her hand. She looked different; rather than the tight black jeans and long leather coat she had been wearing earlier that evening, she was all dressed up now.

Her long gown and pinned up hair reminded her of women depicted in the works of art by Renaissance masters that Italy was so famous for. He had visited many such places with his mother when he was only a boy.

His father had taught him how to fight; his mother had taught him what to fight for.

Even the large empty room they found themselves in reminded of days past. Shiny inlaid marble flooring; dark polished wooden paneling along the walls.

He craved her attention, for those amber eyes of hers to rest on his and let him in.

He accepted her gesture, took her hand, and let his fingers thread through hers. She was cold, so much so it sent a shiver down his own spine.

But he did not let that discourage him. He wrapped his other arm around her shoulder, drawing her in closer until their faces were only a fraction of an inch apart.

He felt her breath tickling his skin. Her lips were so close to his he could almost taste them.

Her eyes shimmered under the crystal chandelier that hung overhead as she looked at him. It wasn't a casual glance; it felt as though they were truly connecting. As though she really saw him for everything he was.

That was when it all changed. Her whole demeanor had taken a U-turn. From confident and stoic, she was now showing vulnerability.

Suddenly she seemed intent on dodging his gaze as much as she had dodged his questions back at the pub.

Lucille was not an easy person to get to know, that much was obvious. She had baggage as well as barriers around her. The walls she had constructed around herself seemed awfully tough to penetrate for someone so young.

What had happened to her to make her this way?

Valentino wanted desperately to find out. He wanted to reach out to her and tell her everything would be all right. That together they could conquer whatever demons lurked in her past and move into a bright future together.

"You should keep your distance," she said, averting her gaze toward the floor.

"I've never been good at doing what I'm supposed to." Valentino smiled and tried to take her hand, only to have her snatch it away. Whatever moment they had shared just now, it was long gone.

Something had changed. As though in that brief second when she had allowed herself to be vulnerable, she had seen something in him that had scared her away.

"The Soul Eater might kill you. I won't able to forgive myself," she whispered.

"He might kill you too. We're in this together," Valentino said.

She shrugged. "I've lived a long life, it's not the same thing. Plus, it's my duty to go after him."

That remark gave Valentino pause. A long life? The girl looked to be in her twenties, younger than he was. What on earth was she talking about?

"It's my duty too. We're both hunters. He is merely our next prey," Valentino argued.

She shook her head. "It's not the same. It's not a fair fight."

He took a step in her direction and reached for her arm again, but was unable to get a hold of her. It was like she had turned to dust at his touch, only to materialize again just out of reach.

"What are you not telling me?" he asked. "I need to

know."

Lucille looked down at her hand. She was holding a dagger; its intricately decorated blade shimmered in the light. Then she looked up at Valentino again.

"There are things between heaven and earth that cannot be explained." She swiftly ran the pointy end of it across her other palm, leaving a trail of blood across her ivory skin.

He was about to shout out in protest, to grab her hand and take the weapon from her before she did anything more drastic, when he looked down and saw that her wound was gone. The dagger, too, had vanished, as though it had never even been there.

"I'm dreaming," Valentino concluded. "This isn't real."

Lucille smiled bleakly. "Just because you're dreaming doesn't mean I'm not telling the truth. If you stay and hunt this vampire with me, you will die."

Valentino paused, remembering the odd phrase she had used earlier. "What's a soul eater?"

Lucille shook her head. "Not everything can be explained. You should go, be safe, live your life."

"And what will you do?" Valentino asked.

"I will do my duty. I will kill him."

CHAPTER FOUR

Lucille paced back and forth outside the Council chambers. Julius had insisted on regular updates, which was fine and well, but that meant she would be forced to come clean about Valentino.

She was secretive by nature and did not easily share her thoughts before she was absolutely certain about them. Inconveniently, she was not yet certain about Valentino Conti.

"Something troubling you?" Dominic, who guarded the door, asked.

She pressed her lips together. Again, opening up in front of other people did not come naturally to her. And least of all with Dominic.

He'd been a guard for the Council since before Julius had appointed her Enforcer. That was over a hundred years ago now.

Unfortunately for him, he wasn't the sharpest pencil in the box. His century or more of loyal service at the Council chamber's doors had earned him no promotion, no progression at all. The only thing he had consistently done that went beyond his duties was try to flirt with Lucille.

She faced him. "Just the entire situation with Marek." This was only partially true. As much as she had been obsessing about finding Marek, she could not get Valentino out of her head either. He had not left her alone, even in her dreams.

Dominic nodded. "That was quite something, wasn't it? How he escaped. Nobody ever saw it coming."

His broad face and build gave away his Slavic heritage, even if his accent was perfectly local. The vampire society in London mirrored humanity perfectly. Sometimes it seemed that half of the people here, Lucille included, were from somewhere else.

Lucille considered his words. Nobody had seen Marek's escape coming. Why not? It was the first time Lucille had come across a Soul Eater of this caliber. She'd been unable to predict that he could break out of the Silver Vault.

"Yes. But why?" she mumbled.

"Why what?" Dominic asked.

Lucille ignored him.

What about the others? The ancients who sat on the Council, including Julius. Had they not known about Marek's immense power? It was a little hard to believe that a vampire like Marek could exist in this world without even one of the elders knowing about it.

That led her thoughts back to the day of the trial itself. She had been so certain that Julius was hiding something. That he and Marek shared some kind of history.

"You shouldn't take it so hard, you know," Dominic said. He reached out for her and tried resting his hand on Lucille's shoulder.

She took a step back and dodged him. Physical contact was highly overrated.

"It's my job to bring him back. I don't have any other choice," Lucille said.

"You don't have to do it on your own, though," Dominic remarked.

Lucille smiled briefly. No, she didn't. Although she wasn't normally a team player, she would have to take all the help she could get. And while her mind was full of doubts and suspicions about why none of the elders had known about the full extent of Marek's powers, who better to help her than someone who had no affiliation with the Council. Who better than a complete outsider.

Valentino Conti.

The only thing left to do was to convince Julius of her plan.

———◆———

"You did what?" Julius bellowed. His loud voice echoed against the cathedral walls, filling every nook and cranny of the space with his outrage. "Why on earth would you share Council secrets with the enemy?"

Lucille stood her ground. She was used to her maker's occasional outbursts. Plus, she was now convinced she had made the right choice. At least for the time being, until she knew who she could trust inside the Council.

"He has no idea who I am. And his methods really are quite revolutionary. I truly believe that together we will be able to track down Marek before he causes more trouble, or even before he flees the city and we may never find him again."

"He's a human, how talented could he possibly be?" Julius scoffed.

"He has scientific methods and equipment I have never come across," Lucille explained.

"And what if he turns his methods and equipment on you and finds out the truth?"

"You overestimate humans, master. They very rarely notice that which they do not want to see. He wants to see me as his peer. To believe that he is not alone in his world. I'm just showing him what he wants."

"You are exposing our secrets, that's what you're doing," Julius grumbled

"I'm not telling him anything he does not already know. He is a hunter after all, a descendent of a long line of hunters. You will have heard of the Conti clan?" Lucille asked.

Julius squinted at her. "The Contis have caused us a lot of trouble over the centuries. Many friends have fallen at their hands."

"Well, he's the last one left. Please trust my judgment and let me utilize his skills."

Although Julius had stopped raging, his expression betrayed that he still disapproved of her idea.

"What if he wants to track Marek at daytime, then what will you do?" Julius probed.

Lucille shrugged. "I've thought of that. I told him I have a job so I can only hunt at night."

"And what if you find Marek together, or run into someone else who knows you and you are exposed?"

Lucille pressed her lips together and took a deep breath. "Then I'll wipe his memory. He is still human, after all," she bluffed. She was not as talented at mind control as some of her peers, but perhaps it would be enough to get by if the worst happened. Provided Valentino did not have access to some kind of high tech defense against vampire hypnosis. Special contact lenses, perhaps. She ought to ask him the next time they met.

Julius slowly shook his head, then gestured at her to come closer. She approached him, her head bowed as a sign of respect.

"My child, understand that I don't want to see you harmed. Marek is a formidable enemy, and putting a hunter in the middle of it all… It's rather risky."

He placed his hand on top of her head. His touch gave her goosebumps, and not in a good way. She only allowed it as a sign of respect.

"I will have Dominic follow you so you'll always have backup when you need it."

Lucille frowned and straightened herself. Julius really did seem concerned. Or was he suspicious? It was sometimes hard to tell the difference with him. She nodded. *Fine, send Dominic after me.*

It would be easy to get rid of him, either by

outsmarting him or placating him with the odd smile and compliment. He had been following her around like a lovesick puppy for a century now. She was certain she could control him.

"I best get back to work," Lucille said. "Marek could be out there raising all kinds of hell."

Julius stared at her in silence for a moment, then waved her away. "Be safe, my child."

Lucille nodded.

She stole a glance at the still shattered stained glass rosette Marek had escaped from, then turned on her heel and left before Julius had the chance to change his mind. As she left the double doors, she could hear him bark instructions at Dominic, followed by rushed footsteps.

Dawn was still a couple of hours away, so Lucille decided to do the one thing she had not yet gotten the chance for ever since Marek's daring escape. She would make a social call. Her destination: an opulent yet familiar villa on Kensington Palace Gardens, belonging to her brother, Alexander.

It had been easy to get rid of Dominic, just as Lucille had predicted. As soon as he realized where she was headed, he had become disinterested in following her. When she told him that her hunt for Marek would continue the following night, he had offered to leave her be of his own accord.

So when she marched through the luxurious entrance

hall and reception room, straight to Alexander's favorite place, the library, she was alone.

"Brother," she greeted the man who sat in his usual spot, one of the brown leather arm chairs, sipping brandy from an old snifter.

"Lucille, what a pleasant surprise," he responded.

She ignored the hint of sarcasm in his tone. Their relationship was cordial, but they weren't particularly close.

"Where's Michael?" she asked.

Alexander shrugged and took another sip. "He moved out last week. Wanted to get a place of his own to share with Anna. They've become very close lately."

Lucille nodded slowly. She had never understood the strange dynamic Alexander and Michael shared, living together in the same house for the last couple of decades. If Michael hadn't been such a notorious womanizer before his run-in with Anna, she might have wondered if perhaps there was something more intimate going on between the two men.

Then again, she couldn't imagine sharing her home, her sanctuary, with anybody. Man or woman. She preferred to come home to blissful silence at the end of the night.

"He'd better be careful, with Marek running rampant in the city. He might want to collect on a grudge or two," Lucille remarked.

"He's quite aware of the situation," Alexander said.

Lucille studied her brother's face.

"I was hoping for your help in this matter."

Alexander straightened himself and folded his hands. "I'm unwilling to put Catherine in any more danger, so you can forget about using her blood to bait him again."

Lucille shook her head. "Not like that; I doubt Marek would fall for the same trick twice. I was hoping to gain some insights into the history and nature of these Soul Eaters. Do you have any relevant materials in this great big library of yours?"

Alexander smiled briefly. "I might do, actually. Over there. Second shelf from the top."

He pointed at a row of old, leather bound volumes.

Lucille fetched the exact book he was talking about and started leafing through it.

"Does Julius know you have these?" she asked.

Alexander shrugged. "He's never asked; I've never told."

"You realize your collection is as comprehensive, if not more so, than the Council archives?" Lucille said. Alexander wasn't easily swayed by flattery, except when it came to his collection of rare books and documents. And perhaps the numerous paintings gracing the walls of his home, but Lucille had precious little appreciation for human arts and crafts.

He smiled again. "It's amazing what you can find when you look in places where the Council, led by our dear maker, won't look."

He was referring to human auction houses, of course. That was where he'd obtained most of his earthly possessions.

Lucille sat down in the empty chair beside her brother. "Where *is* Catherine, actually?" she asked. It had been a while since her last meal, so the temptation of being around a real life Blood Bride might be too much to bear. She might be Alexander's consort and hence off limits to any other vampire, but Catherine's blood was so potent it could tempt anyone into breaking the rules.

"She's resting upstairs. It's been a couple of months, but she is still getting used to her new nocturnal routine."

Lucille nodded. That was safe enough.

Alexander put his now empty glass down and got up to join Lucille. Together they leafed through the book which turned out to be a volume of ancient folk tales from Eastern Europe. Lucille was tempted to say something clever and dismissive, but held her tongue when she came across the first illustration. A spindly figure wrapped in a black, almost cloud-like robe, with long, thin fingers, sharp fangs, and blood red eyes. The creature bore an uncanny resemblance to Marek.

"Not just fairy tales in these books," Alexander commented; he must have picked up on her skepticism earlier.

"Apparently not." Lucille sighed and started to read the accompanying fable about a creature that lived deep underground in a network of tunnels of his own construction, terrorizing travelers and local villagers alike.

It was a tragic tale, which suggested that at least one

powerful Soul Eater had been around for centuries—a reference to Marek himself perhaps? Sadly, it was only the villain himself who'd achieved a happily ever after.

"So. Soul Eaters are invincible," Lucille remarked after shutting the old volume.

Alexander shrugged. "When pitched against poor peasants who can't defend themselves, yes, they are."

"But we're not peasants," Lucille mumbled. *And this is the modern world now.*

"It's obvious then that you need a secret weapon to defeat this foe," Alexander said. "One that the people in this book didn't have."

Lucille looked up and found her brother already staring at her intently.

"And *not* my wife, if you don't mind," he added.

"I think I might have something in mind," Lucille said, getting up abruptly. "Thank you, brother. Our little discourse tonight has given me a lot to think about. Do give my best to Michael when you see him."

Alexander stared at her for a few seconds. "Of course. Good night, dear sister."

Lucille nodded and left without a further word. The information gathered from Alexander's collection wasn't much on the surface of it, but tonight had given her some clarity: much like the creature from the folk tale, Marek did favor hiding underground; he'd even done so the last time she'd captured him with Michael's help.

Furthermore, Marek was an ancient being, set in his

ways and unable to fathom just how much human society—and its technology—had evolved over the centuries.

Valentino, with all his fancy gadgets and know-how, was to be her secret weapon.

CHAPTER FIVE

A hearty meal and strong, yet inferior, cup of coffee helped Valentino shake off the sense of unease that had hung over him since waking up. Those strange dreams that had seemingly plagued him all morning had made him restless. By the end of it all, he was no longer certain if he'd even slept at all or if he'd just been caught up in a persistent hallucination.

Perhaps something he ate? Or more likely…

It had to have been the drinks he'd enjoyed the previous night. He was not used to it, and would need to be more cautious from now on. Hunting vampires was tricky at the best of times; he would need his wits about him.

As he found his bearings inside the unassuming little cafe near his guest house where he'd enjoyed his late breakfast, he had the growing sense that once he met Lucille—after they got to work on their common goal of capturing the vampire—things would fall into place. He could not wait to see her again.

He checked his phone. No messages. Of course not, why would she message him in the middle of the day?

Lucille wouldn't get off work until at least five-thirty, giving them all evening and perhaps a fair portion of the night to start their hunt. It was fitting to hunt a

Nightwalker at night, of course; that was when they were active and you were more likely to come across them. But it did make the whole affair more dangerous. One couldn't simply flee into sunlight if things went wrong.

Still, as long as he had Lucille on his side, they were two against one. Those were already better odds than what Valentino's grandfather had faced all those decades ago. Plus, she seemed to know a thing or two about their common enemy, which would definitely come in handy.

He pulled out his notes and laid them out on the table in front of him.

After they had parted ways the previous night, Valentino had scribbled down a few more thoughts, but there were still a lot of gaps that needed to be filled somehow. Knowledge was power, especially when hunting an enemy this dangerous.

Perhaps tonight Lucille would be willing to share more of what she knew. After all, if he had his reservations about her that first night, it was only sensible to assume she felt the same. Trust was a two-way street, and it only grew slowly.

He sat back and thought again about their conversation at the pub. A lot of Valentino's memories were cloudier than he would have wanted them to be. And what about those strange dreams? Perhaps they were a sign that his subconscious was trying to tell him something that he otherwise would have missed.

One phrase stood out from the fog in his brain, one

phrase he had never heard anyone say before. *Soul Eater.*

Valentino opened a blank page in his little notebook and wrote it on the first line.

Then he opened his laptop and started to research. The message boards and websites he and other hunters frequented were part of what was called the *dark web*. Websites that didn't show up on Google and other search engines.

That made them difficult to navigate, unless you knew exactly where to look. There was no mention of that term anywhere he could find. Perhaps his mind had played a little joke on him and he had simply made the phrase up himself. Perhaps it meant nothing at all.

He sat back and ran his hand through his hair while still staring at the screen.

What the hell, why not?

Valentino opened up a new browser window and typed those two little words into Google. Faced with a million or so search results, which seemed to pertain to an anime series by the same title, he closed his laptop again. Clearly this was just a dead end. He would have seen one of these magazines somewhere, and his mind had fed the title back to him in a crazy, alcohol-fueled dream.

There would be no shortcuts during this hunt. He would have to find the monster the old fashioned way. As soon as Lucille got in touch, the search would be on.

———— ◆ ————

"You made it." Valentino got up from his seat to greet Lucille.

Amazing, how she managed to look so put together and alert after a full day at work, despite their escapades the previous night. Youth had its advantages.

"Of course. No rest for the wicked." She smiled briefly. A rare treat, as Valentino had noticed during the short time they'd spent together. Except when relaxing with a glass of scotch, Lucille was obviously a serious and focused individual.

Perhaps she was warming to his company?

"Where do we begin?" she asked.

Valentino shrugged. "I have not yet worked out where the Nightwalker went after he was spotted near Waterloo."

"I'm sure we can put our heads together and come up with something. What above all else does a Nightwalker require?"

Valentino studied Lucille's face. Her skin was radiant, flawless. Her presence brightened up the surroundings of the rundown cafe where he'd spent most of the evening. Even the other customers couldn't help but steal glances in her direction when they thought nobody was looking.

"Shelter?" Valentino said.

"Right. Especially from sunlight. Luckily for the Nightwalker, London has an extensive network of tunnels, many of which are now disused. I wouldn't be surprised if he was utilizing them to get around the city unseen, as well as stay out of the sun," Lucille said. She pulled a couple of folded sheets of paper out of her coat pocket and arranged them on the table.

Valentino leaned forward and studied the faint maze-like drawings on them. Although the paper was new, signaling it was a copy, the markings beside the plans looked so old fashioned, they had probably been drawn up quite a few years ago.

"Nice. Where did you get these?"

Lucille shrugged. "I know someone who knows someone. There are quite a few public records out there if you know where to look."

Valentino smiled. So she wanted to keep the mystery going. Fine.

"Have you ever been down there, in the tunnels, I mean?"

Lucille sat back and folded her perfectly manicured hands. Had those fingernails ever seen dirt? Valentino doubted it.

"I've explored them a little. There are even underground walking tours for tourists nowadays. Since there haven't been any more suspicious deaths or disappearances in the news lately, it would be safe to conclude that our suspect is being more careful and mostly using the derelict tunnels, not the ones being used for the Underground or sewers."

It would be risky, wandering about in the same tunnels as a dangerous blood sucking vampire.

"Would it not be best to explore the tunnels at daytime? Catch him off guard and perhaps even while he's asleep? We could wait for the weekend, so you don't have to work…"

Lucille brushed away his suggestion. "You underestimate the enormity of this task. Even if we stick only to the abandoned tunnels, that still leaves a huge area for the two of us to search. The chances of running into the Nightwalker on our first try are quite slim. Plus, what do you suggest we do until the weekend? We can't afford to sit idle."

Plus, Soul Eaters don't sleep. Where had this random thought come from? And again, that same phrase: soul eater. He couldn't still be impaired from the night before, could he? Valentino took a deep breath and tried to focus.

Meanwhile, Lucille picked up the plans off the table. She arranged them and folded them in half again, before stuffing them back into her pocket. "If you're not up for it, I'll go in by myself," she said.

"No, no. That's not what I meant." Valentino sighed. She was as stubborn as she was beautiful, this one. And if he was going to be any use at all, he quickly had to snap out of whatever funk he'd woken up in today.

"So it's decided," Lucille said.

Valentino nodded. *Fine.* They'd investigate some tunnels together. For both their sakes, he hoped Lucille was right and they wouldn't stumble across an angry vampire while he wasn't at his best. Judging how she carried herself, Valentino was sure Lucille was a formidable fighter. But would that be enough?

He craved to keep her safe, to protect her, come what may. Funny, to have developed such strong feelings for a woman he had only just met.

------- ◆ -------

Lucille had been correct.

After many hours inside the hidden world that was underground London, they'd found nothing to indicate that the Nightwalker had even been down here. Her hypothesis had made sense, of course, and one glance at Lucille's map also made it painfully clear just how big this task was. Still, Valentino started to wonder if this was all just a waste of time.

"Are you sure he's using the tunnels?" Valentino wondered aloud.

Lucille stopped and turned around. "It's only obvious. It's what I would do."

"Well, okay. But what makes you assume he thinks like you?" he asked.

Valentino wasn't even sure why he was questioning her. But the longer they wandered through these musty tunnels, the more he felt like she was hiding something. Every minute of silence between them had weighed heavier on his mind, and now he had reached breaking point.

"You know something. Something you're not sharing," he said at last.

Lucille cocked her head to the side and pursed her lips.

"You mean like how you're not sharing everything you know?"

So that's how she wanted to play it. Valentino sighed.

"All right. I'll tell you mine if you tell me yours."

Lucille nodded. "That's fair. You go first."

Valentino turned his head and checked the tunnel they had just walked through. It was still as empty as before.

"This vampire. We share a history of sorts," Valentino said.

Lucille nodded. "Me too."

Valentino frowned. So this was personal for both of them. "Here. I have a surveillance photo of him. It's how I tracked him to Waterloo yesterday."

He retrieved the photograph from his messenger bag and handed it to Lucille.

Her expression was unchanged as she looked at it; his appearance had not surprised her. Perhaps she'd even recognized him.

"I have hunted him before, but he got away," Lucille whispered. "His name is Marek."

Valentino nodded. *Marek.* So she did know more about him than she'd let on.

"My grandfather tried to defeat him; or at least, a Nightwalker very much like this one. It was during the time of the Great War," Valentino said.

Lucille frowned as she looked up from the photograph. "He killed your grandfather?"

Valentino shook his head. "He got away. But it was a close call."

That seemed to satisfy her, and she looked down at the still of the shadowy figure again.

"He's not a normal Nightwalker," Lucille whispered.

"You keep hinting at that," Valentino said.

"He feeds not just on the blood of his victims but on their souls," she added.

"A Soul Eater," Valentino blurted out. So his subconscious hadn't tried to trick him. The phrase actually had relevance. Perhaps she had referred to him like this already the other night.

"Yes, a Soul Eater," Lucille confirmed. "And a very powerful one as well. We won't be able to defeat him like a regular vampire."

"No?" Valentino asked.

Lucille shook her head. "The normal ways won't work on him. Silver, for example, will not hold him."

Now they were getting to the heart of the matter. If they couldn't use silver to restrain him, that would make capture very difficult indeed.

"Anything else I should know?" Valentino asked.

Lucille stared at him, the look in her eyes reminding him of one of those strange, feverish dreams he'd had of her. With this reminder came a surge of feelings he couldn't fight. How she stood there, still holding the photograph—it tugged at his heart.

Every fiber of his body was overcome by the instinct to

protect her, to give her whatever she wanted in this world. Right now, it seemed that what she wanted was to defeat Marek the Soul Eater. Good. So did he.

He reached for her and brushed a stray lock of hair out of her face. She flinched, seemingly unwittingly, but stood her ground. Then she looked at him again with those big, dark brown eyes.

"The last person who came close to me died," she whispered.

At least that was what Valentino thought he heard; he couldn't be sure. Perhaps it was just a strange flashback to one of his bizarre dreams.

She handed him the picture and straightened herself. "If we're going to catch this Soul Eater, we have no time to lose," she said, in her old, much firmer tone again.

Gone was the vulnerability she'd shown. Gone was the connection between them. Perhaps he'd just imagined it.

They were back to being colleagues. Nothing less and nothing more.

CHAPTER SIX

After an awkward first night of working together, Lucille had met with Valentino again just after sunset. Together they had planned to investigate the second grid mapped out on her copy of the old underground plans she'd taken from Alexander's collection. If all went well, they planned to cover all of Central London within the week.

As it turned out, they got lucky and found evidence of Marek's activities much sooner than expected.

Marek had only been cautious on the surface. He'd left no obvious evidence for human authorities to find, but if you looked a little further, like Lucille and Valentino had done, there was a wealth of information. It was almost as though Marek intended to be found.

The feeding sites they stumbled across were much fresher than the one near Waterloo; one had been used as recently as a day or so before. Valentino could not detect anything more than that, but Lucille had a few hidden talents.

She could *smell* Marek. She was certain she could track him down there if left to her own devices. So it was time to leave Valentino behind and get the job done on her own.

And so, as soon as Valentino showed signs of tiring, she had feigned fatigue herself and convinced him to call it a night.

Now, less than half an hour later, she was back on her own and ready to follow Marek's trail.

This had always been her biggest talent. Some vampires were good at mind control, some, like Marek himself, had acquired the art of levitation. Lucille was a tracker.

She closed her eyes and breathed in deeply, focusing all her mental abilities on just one thing: identify and separate all the various scents her nose could pick up. Tunnels were tricky in their own way. While above ground human activities often created distractions, down here, it was the pungent smell of human waste that tried to throw her off, as well as the overwhelming aroma of stale blood, courtesy of Marek's unquenchable thirst.

This was precisely the reason Lucille had forced herself to make a pit stop and helped herself to some fresh blood, just before returning to this spot.

She breathed in again, and sure enough, she was able to distinguish Marek's scent from the hotchpotch of stenches that filled the tunnel. It was a very particular smell: old, somewhat musty, with spicy overtones. It was repulsive to her now that she really focused on it. Luckily, that meant it would be easy to follow, even when mixed in with other scents.

As she systematically searched the tunnels with the help of her map, she couldn't stop thinking about the strange partnership she'd fallen into with Valentino.

He made her uncomfortable, but why? He was only

human; a man who had walked this earth maybe thirty, thirty-five years now. She had been around for nearly four-hundred.

It was that look in his eyes, she was certain of it. That look, which made him seem oh so familiar. It had been that same look that had made her forget herself and share everything she knew about Marek the first night.

It had been a very long time since someone had looked at her like that. Dominic, the clingy Council guard, did not count, of course. No, Valentino looked at her not like a meek admirer but as an equal.

Normally, she was good at banishing those old memories from her mind, but tonight, alone in this dark hole in the ground, she was painfully susceptible to them.

These reminders cut right into her core; they made the centuries she had spent as a capable and proud vampire seem insignificant and made her *feel* once again. Lucille hated it. Feelings were messy, terrible things that could overwhelm and make you lose focus.

They reminded her of how weak she used to be. How she had let him down. How she had survived into this new form and he had not.

She had grown up with the boy, back when she was still human in 17th century France. They had been inseparable from an early age, and their friendship had grown into something a lot more intimate as the years went by.

When one of the many religious conflicts that had spread across Europe during those days started to affect life in the formerly peaceful and sleepy village she called home, it changed everything. Suddenly, food was hard to come by. Disease was rampant.

Plague felled many, including her parents, and even the boy she had come to love. Yet somehow, she had survived. That was when Julius had found her and put a heartbroken and listless Lucille back together again.

Tonight, after getting rid of Valentino and continuing her search alone, she wondered if all her strength was just a veneer that hid the old her. And it was this weak and pathetic person that Valentino had once again sought to bring out in her. She couldn't let him; it hurt too deep. Plus, they had no future together anyway. A vampire and a hunter: she couldn't think of a more ridiculous couple.

No, it would be best if she cut their collaboration short and brought Marek to justice as soon as possible. That was what tonight was all about: continuing this quest alone so she wouldn't have to deal with Valentino anymore.

As she turned the corner into yet another tunnel, Marek's scent grew in intensity. She was getting closer. Lucille took a deep breath and did her best to shake off all those idle thoughts about the past. *Focus!*

She wasn't even certain what she was attempting to do here, going after the Soul Eater by herself, but she knew she needed to show strength above all. Her survival depended on it.

Lucille closed her eyes and paused, then she opened them again and scanned the tunnel ahead. It was pitch black and hard to see what lay ahead, even for a mature vampire such as herself; there simply wasn't any ambient light to help her.

Once again, a whiff of Marek's scent seemed to call out to her. He was nearby.

"Come out. I am no threat to you," she said, suddenly extremely aware of the dagger she wore in a sheath on her hip. It would do her no good if they got into a confrontation, though. He was too powerful.

"Marek—" Lucille remembered the formalities he had insisted on during the trial. "Son of Lilith, Master of a Thousand Souls!"

A dark figure approached from the shadows. His movements were smooth and effortless as he levitated a couple of inches off the ground. "So you found me."

She observed him carefully for any sign in his body language that he was prepping for a fight. He seemed perfectly relaxed. *Good.* She had come here for answers, not to be killed.

"I was hoping to speak with you," Lucille started.

The Soul Eater grinned, exposing his razor sharp teeth. "Oh? And what might the both of us have to discuss? Do explain why I shouldn't rip your heart out right here like Julius did with my two progenies?"

Lucille shook her head. Those were questions for another time. Right now, she had to focus on the task at hand.

How had he come to know about the details of how

Julius had killed his associates? Marek had already escaped by the time Julius had jumped into action.

"Because you have no audience. Julius isn't here to see it." Lucille flashed her own fangs briefly. It wasn't a smile as much as an instinctive show of aggression. *Don't show weakness.*

"Very well. Next time, perhaps." Marek made a nonchalant gesture, like he was in no rush.

"I get the feeling that there is more to your relationship with my master than he is inclined to share," Lucille spoke softly.

Marek's gaze locked with hers and the corner of his mouth twitched slightly.

"So you came here to get to the bottom of it all. To find out the truth?" he taunted.

Lucille nodded and averted her eyes downward. "The truth is important to me."

He let out a short laugh and approached her. "All right. It's no secret—not to me. Julius and I have known each other for a very long time. All our lives, almost."

Lucille's mind started digesting the information immediately. All their lives? Julius had never shared the details of his turning and the circumstances under which he'd started his life as a vampire. As a consequence, he had never mentioned Marek either.

"Do you intend to kill Julius and take over the Council?" Lucille wondered aloud.

"Ha! I have no need for that childish Council of yours.

We are vampires. We are eternal. We don't need to be herded like cattle. We are the wolves that roam free: we take what we want, when we want it!"

Lucille frowned. If he had no interest in the Council, then why come to London? Why risk exposure and capture by the Council? Unless… He never actually said he didn't wish to kill Julius, so perhaps that was the plan all along. Get close enough and kill an old rival, simply for the sake of taking his life, rather than gaining any political influence.

"Why stay behind and risk capture?" Lucille pried.

Marek burst into laughter. "Risk capture, you say? Dear child, I'm not risking anything. Your dungeons cannot hold me!"

He had a point, of course. It seemed that the entire period of his imprisonment leading up to the trial itself had been a charade. If the Silver Vault was no match for his powers, he could have broken free at any time. The only ones in danger had been his less powerful associates, and they'd paid heavily for their loyalty to Marek.

Marek reached out for her. His long, claw-like finger approached her face, causing her to flinch away. His pungent scent threatened to overwhelm her.

"Have you ever considered breaking free from all the constraints? All the rules and regulations your precious Council imposes on you? There is a whole world out there, and it's yours for the taking."

Lucille closed her eyes and focused. Was this the end

game, perhaps? Did Marek wish to seduce everyone close to Julius to his own way of life, and *then* kill him after seeing him humiliated?

"I have everything I need right here in London," Lucille said.

"Child, you have no idea of the possibilities. The immense power you could wield if you broke free from the shackles Julius placed on you."

"You mean the power I would gain from killing people?"

"Ah!" Marek made a dismissive gesture. "Anyone can kill. Even humans can kill if they try hard enough. There is nothing special about that."

If she kept him talking, would he share with her the secret behind his great power?

"Then tell me what's special about your way of life. What sets you apart from any old killer?"

Marek let out a hoarse laugh. "I'm afraid if I told you all my secrets, I'd have to kill you. No, you pledge your allegiance to me first, proving your loyalty with a sacrifice of some sort, and then I might teach you."

Lucille considered her options. It would be useful to learn as much as she could. But the sacrifice Marek demanded complicated matters. Considering everything she knew about him, it was bound to be a blood sacrifice. Something drastic enough that she would be disgraced in front of the Council forever.

Unless… It was risky, it was devious.

"What if I told you I could give you a hunter? The one who has been after you?" Lucille said.

Marek grinned. "I was thinking more along the lines of an immortal soul. You offer me a mere human? I can take those for myself any time I want."

"What if I told you he is the descendant of an old foe of yours? A hunter who very nearly killed you many years ago?"

"I do recall a hunter like that… It was during the Great War."

Lucille nodded. "This man I'm referring to is his grandson."

Marek approached her again, his eyes boring into hers. It was a good thing she had been truthful; he would have known if she was lying, she was certain of it.

"Interesting. And you could deliver this hunter to me?"

Lucille swallowed a lump that had been developing in her throat. Guilt? Perhaps even fear?

Would she be willing to use Valentino as bait? It was a risky plan, but perhaps it was the beginning of a plan to defeat Marek. If she gained some further insights into the workings of a Soul Eater, then all the better.

"If you like, I could lure him to you," she said.

"I would enjoy that very much." Marek grinned, exposing his fangs.

"Then we have a deal. I will deliver him to the old industrial complex near the river in Chelsea three nights from now. You know the place; you've been there before."

Lucille gave him a nod, which Marek reciprocated, then turned on her heel. She was half expecting to be stopped, to have Marek swoop down on her and kill her as soon as she turned her back, but he didn't.

He simply let her go.

Perhaps he was underestimating her; Marek was so certain of his superior powers that he did not feel threatened by the prospect of a meeting with Julius' Enforcer and a Vampire Hunter.

Or worse, perhaps *she* had underestimated *him* and their next meeting would end with both Valentino and herself dead in a pool of blood. Only time would tell.

First though, she would have to use all her cunning to convince Valentino to go along with her plan…

CHAPTER SEVEN

A knock on the door alerted Valentino to her arrival.

"Valentino. We must speak," Lucille started, as she marched right past him into his shabby room.

Valentino frowned and shut the door behind her. She looked tenser than usual. Although she had kept her hands buried deep inside her pockets, he could make out that her fists were balled. What had set her off?

"What's wrong?" Valentino asked.

"The Soul Eater. He left us a sign." Lucille retrieved her phone from her pocket and showed it to him. On it there was a photograph of an access door to one of the tunnels they had searched the other night. Only in this picture, there was some writing on top of the dirty gray paint of the door that had not been there before. The red color of the message was so distinctive, it had to have been written in blood.

Valentino Conti, you and I have unfinished business.
Three nights from now, Lots Road, Chelsea.

"I brought you a sample of it to test," she said, handing him a small re-sealable bag with a blood-soaked ear bud in it.

"This wasn't there last night! How did you find it?" Valentino studied the baggie, then looked up and scrutinized Lucille's face.

"Last night after we said our goodbyes, I felt a strange sensation. Like something or someone was calling out to me. I followed it and it led me right back to the door we entered into the tunnels from. Near the most recent feeding site," she explained. "That's when I saw it."

Her eyes were wide, concerned. This Lucille who stood before him tonight was entirely different from the confident fellow hunter he had been dealing with so far. Her experience alone in the tunnel must have really spooked her.

He got to work on the evidence, testing it with his UV torch while Lucille observed. Sure enough, the sample lit up; the blood was definitely contaminated with vampire DNA.

"What do you think it means?" she asked.

Again, two wide eyes stared at him, speaking directly to his protective instincts. He wanted to reassure her, that together they could work this out. Could they, though? The message had come as a surprise even to him.

"Clearly this Nightwalker realizes we're on its trail. Perhaps he was observing us last night. He figured out who I am and that one of my clan hunted him generations ago and intends to even the scales."

"I can guess what you're thinking, but it would be too dangerous to confront him," Lucille said.

She reached out for his hand, and her touch sent an electric shock from her skin into his. The tension between them had only grown since the first night they'd met, and Valentino felt his resolve was close to breaking.

But he had to be strong, for her as well as for himself. The Nightwalker they were after had worked out who he was. The element of surprise in their pursuit was gone now.

"I have no choice. He has challenged me. I must respond."

Lucille blinked a few times, then made eye contact with him again. Her brown eyes were almost black in this light and heavy with emotion. He placed his hand on top of hers and felt her twitch underneath him. This tension, it was mutual. He could feel it.

"Fine. But not without a plan," Lucille said.

Valentino nodded. That was fair. "Yes, we must have a plan."

"And... that's not everything," Lucille said.

"Oh?" Valentino tightened his grip on her hand, squeezing it gently. His heartbeat had sped up; he wanted to touch so much more than just her hand.

"The way I found the message. The way he led me there even though I don't remember seeing him in person. I fear my mind has been compromised."

She still looked unusually fearful.

There had to be an explanation for her strange experience; Marek might have approached her, hypnotized her into forgetting where and how she met with him, and then influenced her to seek out that message for Valentino. It was unlikely that her mind was permanently infiltrated, though.

Valentino smiled at her reassuringly. "Don't worry, Lucille. We'll come up with something."

"Do you know of any way to protect our minds? Do you know how to break the Nightwalker's hypnosis?" Lucille asked.

He shook his head. "Technology cannot help us with that. The only thing we can do is to try and avoid eye contact if we meet one."

Lucille nodded, seemingly satisfied with his answer.

Valentino sat down on one of the creaky old chairs and started to scribble down thoughts and ideas. They needed a plan indeed—a foolproof one. And since Marek the Soul Eater could not be restrained with silver chains or cuffs like normal Nightwalkers, he had to think of something a lot more elaborate. Their adversary was extremely powerful, but he wasn't invincible. Anything that could kill a normal vampire would kill him too, in time.

He reached for the pendant of St. Benedict that hung from the chain around his neck. *Think. What's the way forward here?* He had the knowledge of generations of hunters behind him. But right now, the old ways wouldn't help them. They needed something more powerful to defeat this foe.

"Ultraviolet rays," Valentino mumbled to himself.

"That's it. We will rig up a trap using UV lights. I will be the bait to lure him in, and you set off the lights."

"And what would stop him from simply running away once the lights switch on? It'll take time for the UV rays to kill him," Lucille said.

She was right, but he'd already thought of that. "We'll incapacitate him at the same time."

Lucille frowned. Clearly she did not follow. Why would she? She was an old school hunter; she wouldn't have done the same kind of research he had into how Nightwalkers functioned.

"Nightwalkers are sensitive to electromagnetic waves. If we can create a magnetic field strong enough, it will disorient him and temporarily disable his fast reflexes. Then, we can fight him. It should buy us enough time for the lights to take effect."

Lucille opened her mouth, then closed it without saying anything. Finally, he had rendered his hunting partner speechless. Valentino couldn't help but feel a bit victorious already. Her old school investigative methods and fighting skills and his inventions and research would bring this creature to its knees together. It would be a perfect marriage of old and new, the ultimate partnership.

The brainstorming part of the operation was over; now they just had to assemble the trap and put the plan into action.

He picked up his notebook and stowed it away in his bag. "The meeting is set for three nights from now. If we want to be ready for him, we'd better work quickly. We have some shopping to do."

Lucille's previously surprised expression softened until a subtle smile broke through. "This plan could actually work. I know a few places that should sell everything you need. With a bit of luck, they're still open."

———— ◆ ————

They had managed to find most of what they needed for their trap within the first night. Most of the second night was spent in Valentino's small room, assembling all the bits and pieces and wiring them together. The one remaining night was spent installing the trap in their final location.

And tonight, they would find out if their work would pay off.

Things had been tight, but Valentino felt confident. Even Lucille, who had shown a bit more trepidation at first, had seemingly come around to seeing things his way.

Marek the Soul Eater was overconfident by nature, according to her. And he had no way of knowing about all the technology hunters had at their disposal nowadays. He would not see an ambush of this nature coming.

Now that everything was done, Valentino just had one remaining doubt.

"Are you sure we can place Marek exactly where we need him?" Valentino asked.

Lucille smiled at him, and he felt captivated, unable to

look away from her expressive, seemingly endless eyes.

"He's tried to influence me before; I've had him in my mind," she said. "But it seems like he doesn't want to harm me; at least not yet. He aims to use me to get to you."

Valentino nodded. "And we'll give him what we want." His voice was more monotone than usual—that was how distracted he had become by her gaze.

"Precisely. He's fixated, bordering on obsessed, and that makes him reckless. Once he gets here and realizes where you are, he will simply come to you."

That made perfect sense. Valentino smiled. He was glad to have her here. To be in this partnership.

The longer he looked at her, the more his chest swelled with hope. He had never worked with anyone other than his father during his early hunting days. She'd told him she'd always worked alone too.

Yet now, against all odds, they had made their partnership work. They had complemented each other's talents and become a team.

Tonight was the night when all their efforts came together, and they'd do what they had set out to. Defeat Marek.

Valentino was certain the trap would work; he'd tested it. And once Marek walked right into it, all would fall into place. They would need to hurry, to get into position just in case Marek turned up early. But he still could not look away from her.

"Despite everything, there's still a risk that things could

go wrong, that you get hurt. This could be goodbye," Lucille said.

Valentino shook his head. "No. Our plan will work; I know it."

Lucille briefly glanced away, and he was instantly overcome with dread. *No, don't look away! Everything will be fine as long as I can stare into those eyes of yours!*

She made eye contact again and Valentino's confidence surged. When she reached for him, cradling his face in her hands, his heart skipped a beat.

He instinctively slipped his arm around her waist. This, this was what he had wanted ever since that first meeting at the pub near Waterloo.

She maintained eye contact as she tiptoed and touched her lips against his. It was the most glorious thing. Their first kiss.

It didn't matter that they were about to embark on the most dangerous confrontation of his whole hunting career. He couldn't care less about the stakes they faced. If, by the end of the night, Marek emerged victorious and they were both dead, at least he could take solace knowing they'd lived through this moment first.

If, however, they made it, if they survived tonight, he would ensure that their partnership endured. He would ask her to come home with him; if she couldn't leave London, he'd even consider staying with her. He wouldn't let her go.

Valentino closed his eyes and focused on the sweet

taste of her lips. She was intoxicating, like a drug he'd never known he needed. He'd had his reservations about tracking the Soul Eater to London. That this mission was too dangerous, that he'd put too much pressure on himself to make up for his grandfather's one failure.

But if he hadn't, he would have never met her. He would have never experienced the joy in working with another hunter.

He would have never had this kiss, which meant everything. This connection, which went deeper than anything he'd felt before.

Thanks to Marek's reign of terror on London, he was no longer alone.

CHAPTER EIGHT

Tonight was the night, and hypnotizing Valentino was the last piece of the puzzle. Ever since finding out that he had no gadget to defend himself against hypnosis, she had known that this was what she had to do. Marek expected her to. If he found Valentino fully aware of his surroundings while she delivered him, it would just create suspicion.

Still, she battled conflicting feelings. Although they had done their best to think of all eventualities and built a very impressive trap, the outcome of tonight's encounter was not set in stone. Perhaps Marek had some talents Lucille didn't know about, which would allow him to defeat their trap.

There was only one way of finding out.

She shouldn't have kissed him, though. Kissing Valentino had been a mistake.

Hypnosis was difficult for her; it required a great deal of concentration and eye contact. And as she stared into Valentino's eyes, she kept seeing all those reminders of the past which sought to soften her heart. She had been unable to stop herself.

On top of that, she'd felt all of Valentino's emotions as if they were her own. For a moment there, when she considered that very soon, at least Valentino could be dead, she had lost herself and acted on impulse alone.

And now, the lasting sensation of Valentino's lips on hers made everything worse. She was leading him into danger. He'd agreed to act as bait, sure, but she hadn't exactly been upfront with him.

She'd hidden her true nature from him and allowed him to develop feelings for her, which she felt now that their minds were connected. She'd tricked him into thinking that he wasn't alone in this world, that she was a fellow hunter. As a result, he was ready to make a big change to ensure they could be together. His thoughts had told her as much.

For that, she was sorry.

Lucille took a deep breath. It was too late for regrets; she'd deal with her guilt once this whole sad business was over. Because no matter what the outcome: after tonight, she'd never see Valentino again.

She waited in silence for what felt like forever. Finally, she caught a whiff of Marek's scent. He was here.

"Marek, I'm here with the hunter, as promised," Lucille said as she scanned the large central hall of the old power station. Valentino stood still beside her; he was still lost in his trance.

Memories of their kiss clouded Lucille's mind. She shouldn't have done that. She was dangerously close to losing focus.

Marek approached, floating a couple of inches off the ground as he had done the last time she had seen him. His black eyes bore into hers, as though he could see directly into her most private thoughts.

"Very good. Perhaps Julius' influence hasn't completely corrupted you yet."

Funny, Julius might have said the same thing about Marek's influence. Lucille stole a glance in Valentino's direction; his expression was dazed and vacant. Her hypnosis seemed to be holding. She could only hope that he would snap out of it the very moment she needed him to fight.

Marek circled the two of them, inspecting Valentino from top to bottom. "He does bear a resemblance to that hunter who was after me all those years ago. It never ceases to amaze me how overconfident some humans are," Marek said.

Lucille nodded. "Indeed."

"What about the other part of our bargain?" Marek asked.

"How do I know I can trust you? I've delivered one sacrifice, now I must get something in return before I deliver another."

"Not ready to completely cast off your shackles yet, I see. Very well. I suppose you have done well enough to deserve some kind of reward."

Lucille took a step forward and kept her eyes fixed on Marek's face. "How does it work? What did you mean when you said anyone can kill but what you do is special?"

Marek laughed. "You are suddenly very keen, aren't you? I did not agree to be interrogated."

Lucille glanced away. "Of course not, I am just eager to learn." Eager to learn and eager to buy time. The more distracted Marek was when she initiated the trap, the better their chance of success. And if she could identify what exactly it was that turned a regular vampire into a Soul Eater, even better. Perhaps she could then prevent that sort of thing from happening in future.

The Council had its hands full already with regular criminal elements among their ranks. Lucille would prefer not to have to deal with another Soul Eater as long as she held her position as Enforcer.

"So what is my reward?" Lucille asked as she took a couple of steps in Marek's direction, leaving Valentino behind in the designated spot in the center of the hall.

"I will share with you a little secret," Marek said.

Lucille nodded eagerly. "What's that?"

Marek grinned, exposing his teeth. "You can experience great power beyond your wildest dreams. And its source is right in front of you."

That didn't help. Marek was being vague again, speaking in riddles to confuse her.

"You can give me great power," Lucille said.

Marek nodded. "You could say that. But you must deliver me an immortal soul as a sacrifice."

Again, they were back to that same old story. Perhaps Lucille should just give up on the whole idea of questioning Marek and stick to the plan. It was starting to look like he never meant to share anything meaningful with her in the first place.

"Why would I want to deliver another vampire to you, just so you can take his soul?" Lucille argued.

Marek made a dismissive gesture. "Not just any immortal soul. An important one. The most important one you know."

The nerve. How dare he ask for that? "You expect me to sacrifice Julius? What kind of a demand is that?" she complained. "Do you have any idea how much danger I'll be in if the other elders find out? They'll have my head!"

Marek shrugged. "It's the only way you'll learn about the great power I can give you. But if you don't want that, then suit yourself."

Lucille shook her head. This was it. She wasn't going to get any more useful information out of him. He was too slippery, too suspicious to share anything else before she proved herself. She had no other choice but to end things right now.

"I've brought you the hunter; that's all I'm willing to do for now," she said.

It was time. Lucille kept her eyes fixed on Marek and focused. Mind control was effortless for some of her peers, but for her, it had always been an arduous and tiring task. She was determined not to make her struggle too obvious.

She held her breath and severed the connection between Valentino and herself. He woke up instantly, opened his long coat, and grabbed the axe that had been concealed underneath with one hand, and a short sword with the other. At the same time, Lucille reached for the remote control in her pocket that activated the trap.

The resulting noise was overwhelming. Buzzing surrounded her, infiltrated her mind, slowed her down. She stumbled backwards, trying to get out of the heat of the UV lights, but progress was slow.

The stench of burnt flesh filled the air. The intense pain forced her to her knees.

When she looked up, she could see flashes of Valentino fighting a dazed-looking Marek. Blow for blow, they were equally matched. Valentino's science had panned out; the electromagnetic waves had done their bit in disabling Marek's quick reflexes. He even seemed to be standing on his own two feet rather than floating in the air.

For once, he did not look like the fearsome Soul Eater she had interacted with before, but a frail old man, struggling to stay alive.

Lucille was nearly overcome by pain as the lights continued to burn into her. With tears of blood streaming down her blistered face, she fought her way into the shadows on all fours, where finally she could breathe again.

Meanwhile, Valentino was doing a magnificent job of keeping Marek in the danger zone. He was a great fighter, for a human. Lucille grabbed for her dagger, wishing that she could help somehow. But it was too risky.

She had already endured the lights for too long; her

wounds were only slowly starting to heal. Marek, who had only just begun to smolder, looked like he could still last a bit longer.

But she couldn't just stand there and watch. Her nature didn't allow it. She circled the fighting pair until she stood behind Marek.

Across the room, one of the UV lights went out with a loud pop. The system was getting overloaded; there was no time to lose.

She raised her arm and aimed, trembling as she forced her aching muscles into submission. The din created by the large electromagnet was still slowing her down, disorienting her, but her aim was true. She flung the dagger with as much force as she could muster.

Marek never saw it coming; he had his back turned. Perhaps Valentino didn't either, until the blade found its new home buried deep into the back of Marek's neck. He let out a silent scream and fell onto his hands and knees.

Valentino acted immediately, raised his axe, and brought it down with as much force as he could. That was it, the deciding blow, which severed Marek's head. The Soul Eater slumped to the ground by Valentino's feet. The latter could only watch as Marek turned ashen, then charcoal black, then dissolved into a pile of dust, which was immediately dispersed by a draft blowing through the old building.

At that very moment, the rest of the lights blew out too.

Lucille flipped the switch again before discarding the remote. Finally. She felt like herself again.

She rushed to join Valentino in the center of the hall. It was time for the final stage of the plan.

"Are you all right?" she asked, while staring deeply into his eyes.

Valentino raised his hand and reached for her face. "You're bleeding," he said.

Lucille placed her hand on top of his and shook her head. *Not for long.*

"I'm fine. We did it. Together we defeated him," she said.

It took all of her remaining energy to hypnotize him again. Had he been any other man, she would have fed off him right this moment to regain her strength. But she couldn't bring herself to; that felt like too deep a betrayal of his trust.

"We met Marek, and I set off the trap," Lucille began. "Then we fought him side by side, remember?"

Valentino nodded. "That's how it happened."

As she told him the rest of the fictional account of their battle, she felt her heart grow heavy like before. They had won, but it felt like an empty victory.

This was it. The end.

After tonight, she would never see him again.

Once she was done, she tried to shake his hand, which he refused.

"We'll do it the Italian way, huh?" he said, as he

wrapped his arms around her and kissed her cheek. "Good job, Lucille Amboise."

"Yes… Good job," she said, averting her gaze to disguise the pain she felt.

"Now, I must go. Goodbye."

She turned around and left without looking back. The sting of tears was too fresh. If she stuck around any longer, she might lose her nerve and backtrack on her decision. And that would be bad for everyone involved.

No, this part of the job was done. She had to get back on task and report tonight's events to Julius. They had taken care of Marek against all odds; that ought to please her master. And then, things could finally go back to normal. What a relief that would be.

CHAPTER NINE

Valentino felt conflicted as he reached his modest room at the guest house. With Lucille's help, he had done what he set out to do. The monster was dead. His grandfather's unfinished business had been taken care of. This was cause for celebration, but his heart was not in it.

After all, this meant his collaboration with Lucille was over. She'd made that pretty clear when she left him at the old power station. He hadn't even had the chance to ask her out for celebratory drinks or dinner. Or even breakfast, considering the time.

Did it have to be this way? Were hunters nowadays destined to live solitary lives?

Valentino touched his lips, which still burned with the memory of her kiss.

Just as he settled into the creaky chair in the corner, a rustling noise attracted his attention. He got up to investigate and found an envelope lying by the door.

Valentino quickly opened the door and scanned the dark hallway. It was empty. Whoever had delivered the letter had already left.

He went back inside and picked up the envelope. It was made of some kind of heavy parchment. There was a seal on it, but he did not recognize the symbol on top. It was very old school, the sort of communique his ancestors might have received in the past.

Valentino carefully opened the seal with a knife and took out the folded letter inside.

The handwriting on it was as old fashioned as the paper it was written on.

He carried it back to his chair and started to read.

Mr. Conti,

The woman you have been working with is not who she says she is. You will have picked up the signs, at least subconsciously. Your instincts as a hunter do not lie. She is the enemy.

You owe it to your forefathers, the great hunters that came before you, to take a stand.

Lucille Amboise is not human. She is a Nightwalker.

Remember the oath you, as well as your ancestors, have taken.

You must end her.

Valentino's heart started to race as he read and then re-read those words.

Lies!

He flung the offending letter across the room and rested his head in his hands.

How dare this person interfere? How dare they accuse her of being the very thing they had been hunting together? Had she not proved her worth when they defeated Marek the Soul Eater together? Had she not defended the safety of the human race right alongside him? If the accusation was true, she should have died under those lights, but she'd been fine.

Who could even know about their partnership? Or even his whereabouts? He was cautious, always aiming to blend into the crowd in any new city, yet someone who harbored ill will had followed him here.

Who the hell could know so much about his activities in London?

The letter, like many such tips he and his family had received over the years, was unsigned, of course. People, even those frequenting the same circles as him, were careful about leaving behind evidence of their knowledge about the supernatural for fear of being ridiculed if it was ever discovered. That left only circumstantial clues regarding the sender of this message.

Whoever it was would have been surveilling Valentino and Lucille. Perhaps someone high up in law enforcement or politics? Someone who could have gained access to the many CCTV cameras all around London, like the one near Waterloo which had captured an unsuspecting Marek almost two weeks ago.

But what of its contents?

Surely the accusation could not be true?

Valentino pinched the bridge of his nose and closed his eyes. There was no point in letting his emotions cloud his judgment. He was a hunter, first and foremost. He had a duty to investigate any lead, even a ridiculous one such as this.

What did he really *know* about Lucille?

Precious little.

She was talented with a blade, agile, strong, and quick on her feet. She had razor-sharp instincts and great observational skills. If it wasn't for her, he might have missed out on certain clues pointing them in Marek's direction.

She had been instrumental in the plan to entrap and defeat him.

A lot of it could be explained away. Almost all of it could, except the niggling feeling he had had since the moment he'd met her that there was something she wasn't telling him.

She had a secret.

Had Valentino let his guard down too much? Had he let himself get dazzled by her beauty, by her perhaps feigned solidarity to his cause? Had he let his heart get stolen by the enemy?

He couldn't believe it. It simply wasn't possible.

Only, if this letter was true, that explained a hell of a lot.

Valentino opened his eyes and pulled out his old faithful notebook. In it, he recorded everything he knew about Lucille, aiming to uncover any evidence to prove or disprove the letter's contents.

Their chance meeting inside the pub near Waterloo could have been suspicious. Had she been there because she was also on Marek's trail? Or had she been hunting the hunter and followed *him* there?

They had downed quite a few whiskeys that first night, and yet, she may not have been as affected by them as she should have. This, of course, he could not be certain of, since he had let his own senses get impaired.

She had told him she had a job, so… *He had only ever met her at night.*

This last thought he underlined.

It was still a few hours until dawn; perhaps if he reached out to her, they could put this matter to bed quickly and easily. If he could convince her to meet him during daylight hours, that would be conclusive proof that she wasn't a Nightwalker.

And then he could burn that letter and forget it had ever arrived.

Valentino picked up his phone to dial her number. It rang and rang, but there was no answer. Perhaps she had gone to bed, like a sensible human being should be doing this time of night. Or she was avoiding him after saying her goodbyes already.

He should rest, but he was certain he couldn't relax as long as he didn't have the answers he needed. He had to try to reach her again.

This time, she answered.

———◆———

Lucille watched as Julius paced back and forth in front of her. They had won. Marek had been defeated, so why was he still so agitated?

"There was no way to bring him in alive?" Julius asked, after a seemingly endless silence.

Lucille frowned. She thought he would be happy that Marek was never going to bother them again. His reaction again aroused her suspicion that there was something about their relationship that neither had cared to share with her.

"He made it abundantly clear that our dungeons would never hold him. There was no other viable option."

Julius shook his head.

"It goes against our rules to kill one of our own. Death sentences are meant to be carried out only when following proper procedure."

He was saying one thing, but Lucille heard another. This was not the first time the Council, or one of its representatives, had killed a rogue vampire during capture.

The way Julius talked, it was as though she'd randomly murdered an innocent bystander when this was the very same Marek who was already to be put to death during the trial he escaped from weeks ago.

Even back then, Julius had simply executed Marek's progenies in front of everyone in attendance, as though it was nothing. Nobody had batted an eye.

Suddenly though, when *she* had done the killing—as far as Julius knew; she hadn't told him about the full extent of Valentino's involvement—he almost acted like she had done something wrong. The hypocrisy was getting to her.

"He would have never stopped," she argued. "Do you know why he was in London? Why he came here in the first place?"

Julius stopped pacing and stared at her. "We will never know now. Dead vampires can't talk."

Lucille shook her head. For such a powerful and wise ancient vampire, Julius was being rather thick.

"He was after something, clearly. You knew him well, perhaps you might have some idea what he might have wanted here?" Lucille probed. What could a powerful, ancient vampire possibly be after but more power? And what better source of power for a Soul Eater than a Council consisting of ancient immortal souls, ripe for the taking?

"Why does a criminal, one who broke our most fundamental laws, deserve so much consideration?"

"He..." Julius balled his fists and stared Lucille down

again. His eyes narrowed and a red glimmer appeared in them.

Good, perhaps if he got angry enough, he would let something slip.

"Why won't you understand? He was my brother!"

Lucille was stunned. She had not seen that coming. Despite the hint Marek had dropped that he had known Julius forever…

Vampires generally took after their makers. Julius had taught Lucille everything she knew after he had turned her. Her sense of right and wrong and her belief in the rules they lived by had been spoon-fed into her during her first decades as an immortal. And Alexander was the same; he had his quirks, but he believed in the same ideals. The things Julius had taught them.

There were some exceptions, but that was how it usually went. Some vampires went through a period of rebellion, but it was mostly harmless. Very rarely did a vampire fundamentally betray his or her maker.

Although Julius barely spoke of his early years, she had always assumed that he had been brought up the same. He had never given her any reason to think otherwise. But since Marek had turned out so drastically different, she wondered how true her assumptions really were.

"He was your brother," Lucille whispered. "And because of that you did not wish him to die?"

Julius started pacing again. "It was meant to be me. *I* was meant to end his life."

Lucille was uncertain how to respond; luckily, Julius did not give her much of a chance to.

"I suppose it is time I tell you this, my child. I wished to avenge our maker's death."

Lucille looked up at him, at his once again pale eyes, which seemed to finally show some emotion other than anger. So Marek had killed their maker and Julius felt obligated to take vengeance. That at last made sense.

"Master, I avenged him for you. At least we kept it in the family, so to speak." *In the family indeed.* Thanks to Julius' and Marek's secrecy about their true relationship, Lucille had unwittingly killed her uncle. Not that she felt remorseful about it.

Julius nodded. "In any case, what's done is done."

Lucille didn't respond, but her mind was racing again. Her conversation with Marek, the fact that he had come to London, risking life and limb for *something*… Perhaps Marek had never wanted the ancients' souls. *Perhaps*…

She thought back to something he had hinted at. That if she wanted to experience a power beyond anything she could imagine, she should deliver Julius, sacrifice him.

Perhaps he had not meant to kill Julius himself, perhaps he had intended for her to do it. What if that was the secret?

It made perfect sense.

That little clue was the missing piece of the puzzle. The difference between a vampire who simply murders his prey, and a Soul Eater. In order to become a Soul Eater a vampire must first commit the ultimate sin: parricide. Kill his or her maker.

"Lucille? Are you listening?" Julius demanded.

Lucille looked up. What had she missed?

"Yes, master?"

"The hunter is going to be a problem. A loose end." Julius folded his arms and stared right at her. This was not a suggestion, but an order.

"I took care of him," Lucille said. "He only remembers a perfectly plausible version of events, one that does not implicate me."

Julius cocked his head to the side. "That's immaterial. He needs to be eliminated."

Lucille's chest tightened. *No, he wasn't serious!*

"I can compel him to leave London, never to return. He will not bother us. Plus, he doesn't know anything except that his mission here has been accomplished. The vampire he came here to hunt has been defeated."

"You're not listening to me, child. He is still a hunter. That means he's still the enemy. Why would we willingly let one of our enemies walk away? Especially one with no attachments or family to avenge him. He *is* the last of the Conti clan, as you said. Your sentimentality in this matter is baffling to me."

"He will not be a threat to the Council. To you." Lucille kept her eyes fixed on Julius, looking for any sign that his resolve was wavering. It wasn't. He had made up his mind. And he was very close to losing his patience with her.

"I'd rather not have to repeat myself. You know what you have to do. Those are my orders," Julius insisted.

Lucille nodded, defeated. She had to concede and accept his will. "Yes, master."

In the back of her mind she had always known that involving Valentino in her investigation into Marek carried with it this very risk. But until now, she had never seriously considered the consequences.

Would she be able to carry out Julius' orders? Would she be able to take a human life, Valentino's life? She would soon find out. Julius had left her no other choice.

CHAPTER TEN

The first time Lucille's phone rang, she hadn't picked up. It was Valentino, of course. And for once in her life, she found that she had no idea how to respond to him. What would she say? How would she hide her feelings?

So she had simply turned the ringer off and tried to enjoy the resulting silence. But rather than calm her, the empty house surrounding her and the muted phone in her hand just made her feel cornered. This was not something she was used to. This had always been her sanctuary, her home. This morning, it felt like a trap.

Somehow, Valentino had found a weakness in her and awoken old emotions that had been buried for a long time. Saying goodbye to him had been the most difficult thing she'd ever done, and now, she had to end it forever.

Julius would never change his mind. He could be extremely stubborn, and defying his orders was a dangerous proposition. No, if she valued her role at the Council at all, and wanted to continue living her life the way she had done for centuries, she had to do as he said.

And beating around the bush or delaying the inevitable would not help one bit.

Lucille took a deep breath and picked up her phone to call Valentino back when it rang again.

"Valentino, I was just about to call you," she greeted

him.

The line was quiet; not silent, just quiet. He hadn't said anything yet, but Lucille recognized his breaths on the other end.

"Are you there?" she asked. "Everything all right?"

"I need to see you today. Please tell me you will come."

Lucille frowned and checked the time. Dawn was about two hours away. That was plenty of time to meet up, carry out her orders, and report back to Julius. So long as she stayed focused.

"Where are you?" she asked.

"I'm at the guest house," Valentino responded.

"I can be there in—" Lucille considered what would be a reasonable, human-like, time frame for her journey. "Twenty minutes."

The line went dead with a click. That was very much unlike Valentino. No goodbye, no standard human niceties to end the conversation. Something was definitely off.

She took her time getting ready, though when she left her place, a familiar shadow already lurked across the street, partially concealed behind the trunk of a tree.

"Dominic," she called out.

The shadow froze.

"I can see you, you know. Come out!" she insisted.

Finally, a dejected looking Dominic appeared in front of her.

"I'm sorry, Lucille. I'm here on Julius' orders."

Lucille rested her hands on her hips and kept staring at

the flustered looking man who towered over her.

"I am to follow you, offer assistance during your confrontation with the hunter."

She shook her head. Great. Not only was she being tested with the most difficult task she had ever been ordered to perform, she now had to worry about Dominic meddling in it.

"You will do nothing of the sort," she said.

"But Lucille, those are my orders!" Dominic protested.

Lucille straightened herself and stared him down. Despite everything, she was still his superior as far as Council business was concerned. "I will take care of the hunter myself. Alone. You understand? If Julius makes a fuss, I'll cover for you. But this is something I must do on my own."

Dominic turned away, but then stole a glance at her sideways. "You've never killed a human before, huh?" he asked finally.

Lucille frowned. Why on earth would he say that? Killing humans was against Council law now, but before Julius took over as Council Leader some centuries ago, things hadn't been so strict. Almost every vampire had a few skeletons in his or her closet, literally, so Dominic had no reason to believe Lucille was any different.

"Actually, Dominic, you are mistaken. I *have* killed a human before. That is why I must do this on my own," Lucille explained.

She had never directly ended someone's life, but she'd

felt responsible for so many deaths before Julius found her. The statement felt truthful enough to make her sound convincing.

"Fine, I'll do as you ask. If Julius asks for a report, I'll say that I lost you and couldn't pick up your trail anymore," Dominic said, then he reached for Lucille's arm, patting it; possibly he meant to be supportive.

For a change, she did not dodge him, even if his touch made her feel awkward. Funnily, she had felt a lot less uncomfortable touching Valentino. Was she doomed to live through eternity without ever feeling the joy of sharing a touch or a kiss again? She couldn't even imagine letting Dominic's lips touch hers; the mere idea repulsed her.

"You take care. Remember, he's the enemy. It's all in a good cause," Dominic said.

"Perhaps you were destined to sacrifice him after all."

Lucille nodded, then slipped away into the darkness, leaving Dominic behind.

———◆———

So this was it. Valentino checked the time, then put the phone down. It was a good sign that she had agreed to meet him. But he wouldn't know for sure where he stood unless she stuck around until after sunrise.

They had agreed to meet here, at the guest house. But this was hardly an appropriate place for what potentially had to happen. If he had to act on the mysterious letter, he'd better do it somewhere else. The last thing he needed was to attract the wrong kind of attention by getting into a confrontation in his room.

No, he needed to convince her to accompany him somewhere. Somewhere secluded enough that they would not be disturbed. Somewhere exactly like the tunnels Marek the Soul Eater had used to hide out. Or even the old factory where they'd trapped him. And he needed a good excuse for it so he would not make her suspicious.

That was it. He would tell her he had received an anonymous tip that Marek hadn't acted alone, that there were more Nightwalkers out there that needed to be dispatched.

It was close enough to the truth to sound convincing. And if she was telling the truth, or intent on keeping up appearances, she would not be able to refuse.

Valentino picked up his leather messenger bag off the floor and checked its contents. All of it was still there just as he'd left it: his weapons, his samples, his notes.

Then he sat back and waited. It wouldn't be long before Lucille would arrive and he'd better stay focused and calm.

If the letter was right, he had to be on his guard, but if it was a bunch of lies as he expected, he didn't want to jeopardize the potential for any further relationship with her over some anonymous tip. It was a fine line to walk.

He remained there, sitting on that chair in silence until a knock on the door made him jump up. She was here.

"Lucille? Come in," he said.

She entered, and he could see immediately that she was on her guard. They hadn't known each other long, but he'd never had any trouble gauging her mood right from the start. Right now, as had often been the case, she was tense.

He got up, slung his bag across his shoulder, and met her by the door.

"I have received an anonymous tip. Marek was not the only Nightwalker that needs to be taken care of. The fight is not yet over," he said, all the while observing her expression carefully.

Lucille's eyes met his, and he was surprised at how cold they looked. Her walls were up.

"That's hardly a surprise," she said. "What do you want to do?"

He patted his bag. "Let's properly investigate the old factory, shall we? Collect some samples, analyze the evidence left behind. Perhaps we can find some proof suggesting Marek wasn't working alone."

Lucille pursed her lips. "Sure. Let's go."

Although his suggestion was sensible enough and should not have made Lucille suspicious, the dynamic between them had changed. She seemed to be miles away, as was he. The tension he felt now was no longer one of stifled attraction, but one of distrust.

Valentino wasn't sure how, but Lucille had definitely picked up on the change in him since the arrival of that mysterious letter. Her intuition had always been one of her biggest strengths as far as he could tell.

Or perhaps he wasn't as good a liar as he thought he was.

As they left the guest house and hailed a taxi to take them across the city to the place where their showdown with Marek had gone down, they barely spoke a word. *Just keep it up for a little while. Once the sun rises, we can stop this charade once and for all,* Valentino told himself.

But it was no use. The more time they spent in each other's company, with this painful silence hanging over them, the more on edge he felt.

And the worst part was, she could tell. He could see it written all over her face.

When they finally arrived at their destination in Chelsea, they waited for the taxi to leave and found the gap in the fence where they had entered from before. Still, neither said a word.

Once inside the old, drafty building, Valentino could not contain himself any longer. Her potential betrayal stung too deeply.

"You're not who you say you are," he said.

Lucille approached him so fast he could barely focus on her movements. He took a step backward in shock. Had that just been an optical illusion? It was very dark in here; perhaps that explained it.

"Is that so?"

Valentino fumbled with the buckle on his bag and retrieved his UV torch. He shone it straight in her face, which made her shriek and retreat instantly into the shadows. The air was suddenly heavy with the scent of charred flesh.

That was it. Conclusive evidence.

It was like his chest had been ripped open and his heart removed.

How could he have been so blind, so trusting? And now he had led her here, into this old rotten building, without much preparation at all. Worst of all, he had shown his hand; he had lost the element of surprise.

From his bag, he grabbed the trusty old axe and marched forward, while still holding the torch in his other hand. He had to find her and end this. It had been too good to be true; their partnership was now over. He was destined to take another Nightwalker's head tonight. Lucille's.

"You can't run from me. I'll just keep hunting you down until I catch you," he said.

There was a rustling sound somewhere else in the building, followed by footsteps. He knew it wasn't her. Probably some unfortunate human caught up in their game of cat and mouse. Valentino had been in this business far too long to be fooled by that. Vampires were stealthy; they did not make accidental noise.

He continued on, deeper into the building. Was she still here somewhere, or had she fled?

Something told him she would not run like a coward. They had shared a bond while hunting Marek together. A bond that had cemented itself in his heart during their first kiss.

He could sense that she was still around.

Once he reached the large hall with the old furnace, he tightened his grip on his weapon. There she was, waiting, with a dagger in her hand in the exact spot where the Soul Eater had perished.

Too bad the UV lights had burnt out during their battle with Marek. It would have been so simple to just flip a switch and end things right now.

No matter, this wasn't the first physical confrontation he'd had with a Nightwalker. He wasn't afraid.

Valentino could not believe his monumental failure. How he could have been so gravely mistaken about the woman he'd spent the last week with.

They had hunted Marek side by side. They had worked together like a team. Right up to this moment just now, when all his worst fears had come true, he would have trusted her with his life.

He would have sacrificed everything for her.

And now, they found themselves at odds. She was the enemy, just as the letter had said.

He had let down his family's legacy, everything he stood for. He had let himself get dazzled by a pretty face and the promise of a like-minded companion, and in turn failed as a hunter.

Give up now. You can't win. Valentino wasn't sure if that was his thought or hers. For how long had she been corrupting his thoughts?

He pressed his lips together and stepped forward with his axe raised. He had killed bigger, scarier vampires before. She would be no match for him.

CHAPTER ELEVEN

What were the odds? How on earth had Valentino figured everything out at the exact time Lucille had received orders to kill him? Did it even matter, though? Knowing the finer details of it all would change nothing.

Within the last five minutes or so, they had become enemies and declared war, as it were.

She started to circle him, like a wild lioness, playing with its prey. Although he was a skilled hunter, and no doubt well trained with that axe of his, she wasn't worried. She would win, no doubt.

"This isn't my first fight, Lucille. Give yourself up," Valentino warned her.

She rolled her eyes. It wasn't her first fight either. And she was accustomed to wrangling fellow vampires into submission. A human would be no match at all.

He lashed out with his axe, but she simply dodged him by stepping aside. What was he thinking? Could he not see that there was no hope in hell of him ever winning this fight?

Valentino was tenacious, she had to give him that.

Although her eyes still stung from when he shone his torch in her face, she was as ready for this confrontation as she was ever going to be. All that guilt that she had carried with her tonight had faded into the background now that her life was under threat.

How quickly things changed.

Valentino lashed out again, but she dodged him and retaliated with her own weapon. The shiny dagger with the intricately carved ivory handle had been with her for centuries. A souvenir, from a trip to the Middle East with Julius and Alexander, many years ago.

Although Valentino's reflexes were impressive, for a human, he was not quick enough to evade her. The tip of the dagger pierced his sleeve and sliced into his flesh.

Lucille inhaled deeply. *Blood.*

That must have hurt, but Valentino did not let it show. He stepped forward and swung his axe at Lucille's head, prompting her to hunch onto all fours and jump at him. In one swift move, she struck his hand, breaking his grip on his weapon. The axe fell to the ground, making an almighty racket.

She reached for his throat, and pushed him backwards into the nearest wall.

Her face was only inches away from his, her other hand raised with the tip of her trusty dagger aimed at the side of his neck. With just one jab, she could sever his carotid artery. The blade was sharp enough.

Lucille allowed herself one last look. At the handsome face in front of her. The amber eyes that had looked into hers on so many occasions this past week. The full lips she had kissed just once.

It was too painful. She averted her gaze again.

What on earth was she doing? Their partnership had been like a strange dream, teasing her with possibilities that she had never even considered since the loss of her first love. And this early morning, it had turned into a nightmare.

She inhaled sharply, attempting to force down the painful lump that had developed in her throat, but all that did was bring back even more messy emotions. This fight, this very moment, felt so unreal.

Lucille looked up again and saw not Valentino, but the boy she had loved all those years ago.

Startled, she dropped the dagger, and stepped back.

"I can't. You do whatever you have to, but I can't finish this. You win," she said. Her voice sounded flat and lifeless even to her own ears.

Valentino straightened himself and rubbed his neck where she had just grabbed him.

"I'm a hunter. It's my job."

She shrugged. "Whatever you say."

Lucille observed as Valentino bent down and picked up the dagger she had just discarded. The handle had not survived the fall unscathed; a bit of ivory had chipped off the bottom end. It didn't matter anymore, though. She would soon leave this world and all of her possessions behind.

"You rarely hear of vampire sightings in London," he said, inspecting the weapon in his hands. "How many others are out there?"

Lucille pressed her lips together. She might have capitulated, but she wouldn't tell him any more Council secrets.

"How do you keep your activities under wraps? Or are there so many unwanted people out there that nobody cares to figure out what happens to them when they disappear?"

She shot him an angry look. "If you must know, we don't kill."

Valentino paused. "Vampires that don't kill. Now there's something you don't hear about every day."

"There are plenty of things you know nothing about," Lucille snapped.

He was getting to her. Why was she allowing herself to be goaded into answering these inane questions? She ought to just keep quiet and wait for the inevitable. At least then her heart would stop hurting.

Valentino took a step towards her and Lucille closed her eyes and braced herself.

"If you had wanted to kill me, you could have done so on numerous occasions. What changed?"

She balled her fists and stood her ground. *Enough*. She would say no more.

"Someone ordered it, right? That's what's different now. And now you'd rather give yourself up than face the consequences of disobeying that order."

She shook her head. He would get nothing else out of her.

"Don't worry, I'm here to help," another male voice startled her. Dominic.

Bloody hell, so he had ignored her instructions and followed her anyway! Lucille opened her eyes and just about caught a glimpse of the other vampire charging toward Valentino.

Lucille did not get time to think, only act. Before Dominic had the chance to hurt Valentino, she was on him, clawing at the flesh on his shoulders and biting into his neck. A steady trickle of fresh blood entered her mouth. Clearly, he'd fed sometime tonight.

She dug her fingernails deeper into his shoulders and dragged him backwards into the next room.

Dominic should have just stayed away like she'd told him. He would regret his insubordination dearly.

"Don't you dare," she hissed in his ear. "Don't you dare attack him."

"But he was about to kill you!" Dominic argued. "And he murdered Marek. He must pay for that!"

"I was handling it!"

Lucille forced Dominic down onto the ground. Despite her smaller frame, Lucille was quite a bit stronger than she looked. Dominic was a much younger vampire and still had a lot to learn.

She glared at him and let his earlier words sink in. The realization hit her like a brick wall. He knew Valentino killed Marek even though she'd never reported that detail to Julius; fine, so he'd followed her earlier. But the thing he'd said back at her house about sacrificing Valentino…

There was no reasonable way for him to know about that. *Unless...*

"If you don't back off right this minute, I'll tell Julius that you've been colluding with the Soul Eater."

Dominic's eyes widened in shock. So she'd guessed correctly.

"I was only trying to help... I'm... I'm so sorry!" he mumbled.

"As you should be. Now bugger off and let me handle the hunter!" Lucille barked.

She got off him and Dominic reluctantly stood up and backed away.

"Go! I'm not going to tell you again!" she called after him.

Lucille waited until he was out of sight. It would be so easy to just leave as well, if only her pride didn't prevent it. She had already failed to carry out her orders and it was only a matter of time before Julius found out about it. The life as Council Enforcer that she had become accustomed to was now over.

She had let Julius down.

Footsteps approached, dragging her back to reality.

"Lucille," Valentino called out.

"Yeah. I'm here," she said as she sat down on top of a pile of rubble in the center of the room.

He approached her with his arm outstretched and her dagger in his hand.

"I can't do it either."

They stared into each other's eyes as she accepted the weapon. There was so much there to see. For Lucille, it was all a painful déjà vu.

"What a pair we are, huh? Sworn enemies. Yet we cannot bring ourselves to kill each other," Valentino remarked. There was a sad glint in his eyes.

"I suppose life isn't always black and white," Lucille said. Funny that she was the one uttering this phrase now. Just two weeks ago, she would have passionately disagreed with that statement. Lucille had spent centuries as a stickler for the rules.

And now, for the first time ever, she found herself stuck in the gray areas of life.

"I've never met a woman like you," Valentino said.

Lucille looked up at him again. Could she give this up? Could she give *him* up?

"This can never work," she said.

Who was she trying to convince exactly? The little voice in the back of her head tried to disagree vehemently. So what if he was a hunter and she was a vampire?

"My forefathers would be spinning in their graves if they saw us now." Valentino averted his gaze and started to pace back and forth in front of her.

"I attacked one of my own. I can't believe I did that."

"He seemed pretty surprised too," Valentino remarked.

"Oh, you noticed that, did you?"

Dominic's reaction had been almost funny, if their circumstances weren't so tragic. Still, Lucille found a little smile creeping over her face. She looked at Valentino, whose expression had softened as well. Then, her smile turned into a giggle, before erupting into laughter.

Valentino sat down next to her and joined in.

The pain, the confusion was too much to bear. Next thing she knew, her face was wet. At some point, without realizing it, she had stopped laughing and started crying.

***

The other vampire had come out of nowhere. Valentino was not prepared at all and very nearly paid the price. He also was not prepared for Lucille's reaction. Within the blink of an eye, she had taken care of the threat and dragged Valentino's assailant backwards out of view. For an experienced hunter, he had really let his guard down one too many times tonight.

Of course he'd gone after her, searching through the adjacent rooms and halls. When he found her, she was sitting on top of the remnants of a concrete support beam that looked like it had fallen from the ceiling of the old building a long time ago. As he observed her sitting there, hunched over with her head hanging down in defeat, he could not take it anymore.

He'd never planned for this moment. From the moment he'd read that letter, he'd hung on to the assumption that it was full of lies. And although discovering the opposite had shocked him deeply, he could no longer bring himself to hate her.

They spoke in fragments and statements that didn't

make a lot of sense. He'd offered her the weapon he'd picked up as a gesture of goodwill.

She accepted his gesture, her face tense with regret.

She was the enemy. He was meant to kill her.

But if she was really a monster like those he'd hunted before, even like Marek whom they had defeated together, she wouldn't have surrendered to him. She would have finished the job before he had the chance to defend himself.

He told her he'd never met anyone like her.

She responded that it wouldn't work.

They stared into each other's eyes and he wondered if she really meant it.

These were not the eyes of a dangerous monster. Evil was supposed to be ugly, repulsive, but he'd never seen any of that in her. Not when they'd worked together, and not now.

He remembered what she'd said only moments ago, that she did not kill humans. Her actions had proved as much. That in itself meant she was different.

Valentino had always been so proud of his heritage. Vampire hunters for generations. He'd grown up with stories of his forefathers' conquests. He'd gone on hunts with his father once he was old enough.

Never did he consider that he still had so much to learn.

"I attacked one of my own. I can't believe I did that," she said.

"He seemed pretty surprised too," Valentino quipped.

"Oh, you noticed that, did you?"

She laughed. It was the first time she'd really let loose in front of him. It was contagious, so when he sat down next to her, he soon found himself joining in.

He glanced at her and noticed tears streaming down her face.

Enough. To hell with the old rules.

He put his arm around her and pulled her close.

They had hit this roadblock together. While he found himself doubting everything he'd ever believed in, she was facing a similar crisis. They didn't need to face it alone.

Despite everything, they had proved their loyalty to each other already. That had to mean something.

Valentino closed his eyes and buried his face in Lucille's hair. She did not resist him, quite the opposite. So they continued to sit there in silence, in that cold, drafty old power station, their arms wrapped around each other.

If everything went wrong tomorrow, if they never saw each other again, at least they'd had this moment together.

CHAPTER TWELVE

They had stayed at the old power station until the approaching dawn had made itself known to Lucille. Neither his room at the old guest house nor her home would be safe. Julius would know to look there.

They found refuge in the one place everyone who defied the Council seemed to flock to. Alexander's villa.

The latter had not been impressed to find Lucille and a bruised stranger on his doorstep at six in the morning. But with twilight already upon them, he had not been so cruel as to send her away.

"Just for one night," she'd insisted. "Then we'll be out of your hair."

He'd shrugged and retreated back inside and up the stairs. "You'll do whatever you want anyway."

Now Lucille found herself alone with Valentino in one of the spare bedrooms, where they looked painfully out of place. Dusty, torn clothes and dirt smudged skin stood out against the opulent Regency decor Alexander loved so much.

What on earth was she doing here? With a human—no, a *hunter*—who had a prize on his head.

No wonder Alexander's greeting had been even colder than usual.

"Perhaps we should talk," Lucille began.

Valentino stopped inspecting the room and focused on her instead.

"How much of it was true?" he asked.

Lucille sighed. She knew this part of the conversation would be inevitable.

"I hypnotized you earlier. Before we fought Marek."

Valentino nodded. "I suspected as much. But which memories are false?"

Lucille took both of Valentino's hands and made eye contact with him.

She wasn't sure this would work, but she at least had to try and undo the damage she'd done to his memory earlier. It was the least she could do.

She focused all her energy on releasing those events from the past few hours that she had previously blocked access to. Once that was done, she also transferred some of her own memories and knowledge: her private interactions with Marek, and her last report to Julius.

Valentino blinked a few times and frowned. It was a lot to process, no doubt.

"Wow," he said, when Lucille severed their connection again.

She brushed herself off as best she could, then sat down, gingerly, on the edge of the settee.

"I'm sorry. I was just trying to defeat Marek. And I had to protect my secret," Lucille whispered.

Valentino shook his head. "It's not that. I'm actually surprised at how much I remember correctly."

"What do you mean?" Lucille looked up in surprise.

"The kiss. I half expected that to be an illusion."

"Ah." She sighed. "Yeah, that really happened. You were meant to be under my control at the time, but I fear I might have been influenced by you in return."

"But you meant it?" he asked.

Lucille folded her hands in her lap and stared down at them. Had she? The urge had overwhelmed her and made her lose control of her own impulses and emotions. Of course she'd meant it. But the secret was out now. Surely, his feelings for her would have changed?

She looked up and found Valentino already staring at her. "Did I want to kiss you? Yes. Do I think it was a good idea? No."

He shrugged. "Who is to say whether an idea is good or bad, as long as it feels right?"

She frowned. Valentino was full of surprises.

"So how did you find out about my secret?" Lucille asked.

Valentino retrieved a piece of paper from his messenger bag and handed it to her. She got up to accept it.

It was an envelope with a broken black seal on top.

Lucille stared at the offending document and found that her knees were getting weak. The seal was different from anything she'd seen before, but the paper was so distinctive she would recognize it anywhere. It wasn't just the quality, the texture of it, but also the scent. She'd received communications like this before. And they had always come from the same sender.

She opened it with trembling fingers and pulled out the parchment inside. The handwriting was equally distinctive.

Julius.

"I don't believe it," she whispered.

She crushed the paper into a ball and flung it across the room.

Valentino came up behind her and rested his hand on her shoulder. "That's pretty much how I reacted too."

She spun around and looked at the man she'd very nearly hurt, and worse, almost killed. It shouldn't have come as a surprise that her own orders to eliminate Valentino should coincide with a similar directive sent to him. Julius liked to play it safe; why shouldn't he hedge his bets?

If Julius suspected Lucille might disobey, at least Valentino might follow through and force her hand, thus ensuring that his will was done. It was only sensible, and yet it felt like a deep betrayal.

Julius never ran his own errands, so Dominic was undoubtedly involved. And he had been there at the power station, watching when Lucille laid down her weapon. Even if she could continue to blackmail Dominic into helping her, there was no hope. Julius was too suspicious by nature; he would insist on seeing a body.

"My maker sent this. *Julius* sent this," Lucille said. The game was up. What were they going to do?

Valentino frowned. "Why would your maker want to see you harmed?"

Lucille shook her head. "You don't understand. He didn't expect for you to succeed. He was just trying to make sure that I'd be forced to kill you. If not on his direct orders, then at least in self-defense."

Valentino smiled. "Seems he underestimated the two of us."

Lucille started to pace around the room, back and forth, again and again. Now what? Defying Council orders was a grave crime. He would try to punish her, and then execute Valentino anyway as an enemy to vampire kind. She had come too far to defend him already; she had to find a way not to let that happen.

"He will kill you. He might even kill me for disobeying him."

Lucille sat down on the settee again and rested her head in her hands. *Think! What's the most logical way out of this?*

"I suppose killing him is out of the question?" Valentino asked.

Lucille shot him a disapproving look. "He's still my maker. He's been like a father to me for centuries." Plus, if she did that, she suspected she'd turn into the very thing they had been hunting together: a Soul Eater.

Valentino nodded. "Fair enough. So how about we just go? Leave this place and everyone in it. He has his responsibilities here, doesn't he? So he's unlikely to come after us?"

Lucille was about to protest. London had been her home for so long, it was hard to imagine anything else. But Valentino did make an excellent point. Julius was much too suspicious about being superseded if he left the Council behind to hunt after her.

"You want me to run away with you, after everything that's happened? After everything I've done to you?" she asked.

"Perhaps I've been alone for too long," he said, with a grave expression on his face.

"You realize I've been on my own for four-hundred years, right?" she asked.

Valentino grinned at her. "Fair point. But I imagine the years pass much quicker when you're immortal."

"Touché."

"Come on, think about it. We'll make a fresh start. I'll take you home to Italy. It's a beautiful country, you'll see. And the food is amazing…" Valentino's expression fell again. "Wait, can you eat human food?"

It was Lucille's turn to grin. "Of course. But I'll still need the occasional dose of fresh blood to sustain me."

The relief was evident on Valentino's face. "Thank God. I can't imagine spending a lot of time with someone who doesn't appreciate a good meal."

Lucille couldn't stop herself from staring at him. Was this it? Was this love? Normally it annoyed her when people behaved in ways she couldn't understand. She should find his quirks irritating, but instead, he intrigued her.

She wasn't quite sure what outcome she'd intended when she refused to carry out Julius' orders. She'd been ready to lay down her life to protect Valentino, but she hadn't actually considered the possibility of *being with him*. Now that they were alone, her mind was trying to play catch up with what her heart had wanted all along.

Here he was, despite everything, trying to convince her to what—elope with him? What a strange man he was. A beautiful optimist who despite everything, was still trying to see a positive outcome at the end of it all.

Her heart surged when she thought about it. Should she risk it? For once in her life, should she stop thinking with her head and just jump into something, no matter how silly and ill-advised it was?

"You know, this might actually work," she mumbled. And if they left together, she wouldn't have to involve Alexander any longer than necessary either.

"Of course it'll work. As long as we both want it to," Valentino urged. "I know you tried to yourself, but I am not ready to say goodbye."

There it was again, that look. The one that had sought to disarm her from the start of their partnership. The one that brought with it so much baggage and uncovered so many scars she thought had faded centuries ago.

Lucille pressed her lips together.

Valentino sat down beside her and put his arm around

her, just like he had done at the old power plant. The gesture gave her shivers, in a good way. It sent a warm rush down her spine that filled her heart with hope.

Surely she didn't deserve this man and everything he was trying to offer her?

His hand traveled up her back until it reached the nape of her neck.

"What do you say then?" he whispered.

His voice, so smooth, it was like warm honey. And his scent… A lot had happened since their first kiss; would it still feel the same?

Lucille reached for him, embracing him and bringing their faces closer together.

She sought out his lips with hers and closed her eyes when he bridged the gap, kissing her with a passion they hadn't shared before.

Words couldn't describe what they shared now. This bond, this understanding. All of Lucille's worries and fears faded into nothingness and all that mattered now was that they were together. This was what she had needed all along. For someone to come and chip away at her hardened exterior until the old her re-emerged.

She was no longer Lucille, stern and cynical Enforcer of the Council of London. She was just a girl. A girl who had come from simple beginnings in 17th century France. A girl who fell in love with her best friend and then promptly lost him and everyone else she cared for.

For the umpteenth time tonight, tears streamed down

her face. Only this time, they were happy tears.

Even those memories she had buried so deeply for hundreds of years seemed to not matter anymore. This, this moment right here, with Valentino, was all that held any importance to her. She felt relieved, redeemed. She had risen from her own ashes.

Without even realizing what he'd done, this man from a world so different from her own had given her a second chance.

Their second kiss *didn't* feel the same. It was infinitely better.

CHAPTER THIRTEEN

Valentino felt like he had woken up in the middle of a dream.

In his arms was a woman unlike any he'd met before. A flawless beauty, whose complexion was so perfect it could have been carved out of the finest Italian marble. During most of their past interactions, she had shown herself to act cold as well, but this last hour or so with her had changed everything.

Her eyes were no longer guarded. Her touch was filled with heat. And her lips…

Valentino had never known a taste more intoxicating.

Had someone told him even just two weeks ago that he would find himself here, in a strange vampire's house, making out with said vampire's sister, he wouldn't even have laughed. He might have been tempted to cut the messenger's head off.

But this wasn't an illusion. What they shared was real. And as bizarre as it was, he felt strangely at peace with how things had turned out between them.

So not all vampires were monstrous killers. They needed blood to survive, but some had found more ethical ways of procuring it than simply taking human lives for it. That had made his decision to fight for a chance with Lucille a lot easier.

There would be a period of adjustment, of course. Save for one miserable attempt in the past to let someone into his life, he had been a loner. Women had come and gone, but none had left a lasting impression.

And the same was true for Lucille as well, who had spent centuries on her own.

But ever since she'd surrendered to him earlier tonight, he knew that this was the right way forward. Against all odds, they shared something. Call it a connection, a sense of solidarity. Love?

In addition to that, they also shared a heavy dose of something more primal in nature. Passion, lust, whatever you wanted to call it. Lucille and Valentino had heaps of it.

They'd been dancing around each other for only a week, but what felt like a lifetime of frustration was about to be cast off in a most spectacular fashion. He was ready for her.

Of course they'd done this before, briefly. The memory of their first kiss was still fresh in Valentino's memory. He'd been under her influence at the time, but even that could not taint his perception of it. He'd been wanting to kiss those shapely lips from the moment he'd first laid eyes on them. To know she'd felt the same was too precious to let something as petty as their circumstances or opposing backgrounds get in the way of it.

Every touch of hers now felt like a lifeline to keep him from drowning. The events of tonight had changed his outlook in life. Beliefs he had held on to all his life were shattered. Future plans that he had considered certainties had been discarded.

He was ready to wipe the slate clean, to break free from his past and his legacy in order to rediscover a new life with her.

Valentino closed his eyes as he let his hands roam her body. It didn't make a difference. Eyes open or closed, he could see only her. She filled his mind, his soul, his whole being.

She pulled away, just for a moment, prompting him to chase after her.

Lucille stood in the center of the room, beckoning him to come closer. He couldn't refuse if he tried.

He tore at his clothes, ridding himself of every last barrier that could get in their way.

Lucille followed his example. Even his wildest dreams couldn't have compared him for the vision of womanhood that stood before him. He wasn't sure what he was expecting, but it wasn't this. She looked radiant, alive.

"Take me. Make me yours," she whispered. Or perhaps that was just what he wanted her to say.

It made no difference. His desires or hers, they were the same.

He reached for her, only to have her dodge his touch and edge her way backward to the bed.

No, not there. He wished to have her here on the floor.

And against the wall.

And on the sofa.

And…

She smiled seductively, then vanished into thin air, only to reappear behind him. She wrapped her arms around his waist, running her long fingernails over his chest and stomach, stopping just short of his cock. Oh, the sweet torture.

"I'm rather used to being in charge. I hope you don't mind." Lucille kissed him just below the ear, which sent a fresh surge of desire right through him.

Valentino shook his head. "Any way you want this is fine by me."

He turned around and wrapped his arms around her. She leaned into his embrace, then immediately flinched away and let out a loud shriek. Something had caused her to cry out in pain.

"What happened? What's wrong?" he asked. Valentino's heart beat surged. What had he done? How could he make it better?

Lucille pointed at his neck and his heart sank. *How could he have forgotten about that?* Valentino reached for the chain around his neck. His pendant, the medal of St. Benedict, was made of silver. No wonder she'd reacted the way she did upon touching it.

He tugged at it in anger, breaking the chain and throwing it as far away from them as possible.

This token had been with him forever, and although he never believed in its supposed supernatural powers, it had been a support to him in the past. A reminder of his heritage and a crutch to help him follow in their footsteps. But the meaning he'd attached to it was well and truly tainted now.

His forefathers wouldn't have asked questions or tried to understand. They would have taken Lucille's head off without hesitation. He didn't want to belong to that world anymore. How could he?

"I'm so sorry," he whispered as he pulled Lucille back into his arms. "I didn't think."

She shook her head. "It's fine. I'm a fast healer."

As soon as he felt her naked body against his again, their passions flared up as though they'd never been interrupted. She dug her fingernails into his shoulders and he groaned in sweet pain. He needed to show her just how much he wanted her. His body, his heart demanded it.

It was a strange realization to know that the woman he was with right now could tear him limb from limb if she chose to. And yet that did not intimidate him; it only made him want her more.

She jumped him, wrapping her lean legs around his waist.

With any other partner Valentino would have expected a good amount of foreplay, but Lucille seemed unwilling to wait. Their desires were too urgent to be ignored any longer.

Valentino held on to her hips, marveling at the firm curvature of her ass. So this was what a warrior's body felt like. He stumbled straight across the room, until he had her pinned up against the nearest wall.

Then he entered her. Their kiss earlier had seemed like the most glorious thing ever, but this exceeded it thousand fold. Lucille moaned loudly as he started to move.

How tight she was. How perfect.

Her fingernails dug into his back now, not hard enough to pierce skin, but just right to hit the perfect balance between pleasure and pain.

It was like she knew exactly what he wanted and how he wanted it. Similarly, he seemed to know just what she needed him to do. She would like it faster, more forceful; his instincts told him so.

He did his best to deliver, burying his manhood into her repeatedly, as deep as he could go.

Her body responded by gyrating into him, egging him on, faster and faster.

Valentino's chest felt ready to burst. His throat tight. He had so much to tell her, but his actions seemed inadequate. Faster and faster he went, eliciting more moans and muttered encouragements from her lips.

He was only human, and she was so much more. Would he satisfy her?

Beads of sweat started to appear on his forehead as he fought through the beginnings of his fatigue to make her happy. Just when he thought he'd reached the end of his reserves, something made him push through and find further strength.

That was what her influence did to him. She challenged

him; made him want to be better—stronger—than he really was. This was it, the essence of his attraction to her. It was what made him fall for her despite himself.

"Oh, God, I love you," Valentino gasped. He had blurted it out just like that, without considering her reaction.

Lucille grabbed a handful of his hair and pulled his head back to expose his neck. She ran her tongue across the whole side of his neck, then stopped just below his ear.

"I love you too," she whispered.

He closed his eyes, savoring those words she said. This, of course, wasn't a fairytale kind of love. He wasn't her white knight, and she wasn't an innocent maiden in need of rescue. They had both lived a life of darkness, in a way. They were well versed in the language of violence and death.

It wasn't a surprise then that what they were doing right now wasn't lovemaking. It was feral, unapologetic, and carnal. They all but fought for pleasure, not just for themselves but for each other.

He wouldn't have it any other way.

"Drink from me if you want," he said.

"I thought you'd never ask."

As Lucille bit down into his neck, he was overcome with yet another intense sensation he'd never felt before. It was like all the orgasms he'd ever felt in his life rolled into one. It was painful and infinitely pleasurable all at once.

She pulled back and cried out. Her body writhed and

spasmed against his rigid arms. He could barely hold on.

This was everything they'd battled towards, the pinnacle, the peak of their release. Every muscle in her body seemed intent on keeping him buried inside her and squeezing every last drop of pleasure out of him.

It took him a few moments to catch his breath. Lucille, of course, had no such trouble; her stamina vastly outpaced him. Still, the sun was probably up already, and her eyes betrayed that she was getting worn out too.

Valentino carried her to the bed and got in between the sheets with her still clinging on to his neck. Finally, as they were enveloped by the soft mattress, he felt her tense muscles relax.

"Tired?" he asked.

"Maybe," she said.

Although she lay in his arms now, Valentino had a feeling this would be a rare treat. Lucille didn't seem like the cuddling kind. And that was just as well, because neither was he.

She traced her fingertip along the outlines of one of the many scars that covered his hardened body. He didn't mind. He wasn't ashamed of any of it.

"Where did you get this one?" she asked.

He looked down at the star shaped mark on his chest. "Romania, 2008. While I was hunting a Nightwalker who had recently killed an entire family of locals, the police mistook me for the suspect and shot me."

Lucille nodded. "I've been shot before. It stings."

Valentino chuckled. "It did a bit more than sting. I almost didn't make it."

She raised her head, her eyebrows pulled together in concern. "I have a way around that, you know."

"What do you mean?"

Lucille pursed her lips. "Well, if we're going to do this—be together, I mean—we could make it official."

"What, like marriage?" Valentino raised himself up on his elbows and looked at her. Growing up, he wanted nothing more than to settle down with someone. To have the kind of companionship and love his parents had shared. He'd never figured Lucille would want the same.

"Well, sort of. If we do that, your life will be bound to mine. You'll still be human, but you'll live as long as I do. You'll stop aging. You'll be safe from harm." The way she looked at him now with those big, brown eyes stirred something up in him. She didn't need his protection of course, but nobody had told Valentino's instincts that.

He nodded. "If you'll have me."

Lucille smiled, the relief evident in her eyes. "I don't think I could bear if I lost you now. Not again."

"Again? You'll have to explain that one to me."

Lucille lay her head on his chest again and took his hand. "It was a long time ago. At first I thought you reminded me of him, but then I realized that you're nothing alike. I was simply reminded of a feeling I had before."

Valentino settled back into the pillows and closed his

eyes as he listened to her story.

The longer she spoke, the more he felt like he finally understood.

There were no more secrets between them.

EPILOGUE

14th February
Valentine's Day

It was a beautiful ceremony, conducted by Lucille's brother, Alexander, in a most scenic setting.

Valentino's family had owned this villa that stood proudly on top of a barren hilltop in the Italian Alps for many generations. He had inherited it after his father's passing two years ago.

And on a clear and desolate night like tonight, it was mostly the stars overhead that acted as witnesses to Lucille and Valentino's wedding. They stood bathed in moonlight, filled with hope for their shared future.

The ritual ended with the two of them holding hands after making the blood sacrifice necessary to cement their relationship. And now when she looked at Valentino, she could she a subtle glow surrounding him. Their bond had taken. He was now hers, as she was his. In life, in death, until the end of days. Although humans couldn't see it, any respectable vampire would know that Valentino belonged to one of their own and be unable to harm him. The laws they lived by forbade it.

They shared a kiss, then Lucille excused herself to take care of the rest of the arrangements. Valentino never insisted on it, but she knew an Italian wedding was never complete without a feast fit for kings. Lucille had wanted to make sure that everything was just as it should be.

As she returned with one of the many dishes she'd procured—actually cooking the food would have just resulted in disaster—she stood and watched Valentino, who was now chatting to Alexander. It was a strange sight: the man she'd chosen to be with making friendly small talk with the one who had been a companion of sorts for the longest time, at least during the early days of their turning.

They seemed to get along, which made Lucille smile. Not that she cared if her brother approved of her choices; she was way too strong-willed for that. But it made the scene look strangely normal. A new husband chatting to his brother-in-law.

Lucille thought back to what it had taken for them to end up here. All the trials she and Valentino had been through. How she had hidden her true self from him, deceived him, and tried to use his expertise for her own purposes. How he had forgiven her for all that and convinced her to come here.

They had escaped London in the dead of night, and with it, Julius' wrath. Although Valentino would be safe from harm now that they were wedded, the same protection didn't extend to her; she still had defied official Council orders. There were consequences to that sort of thing.

Lucille diverted her attention away from her other half

and toward her brother. It had surprised her that Alexander agreed to come. After turning up on his doorstep with Valentino during their last night in London, she almost expected he wouldn't want to get involved in this whole affair. He had already angered Julius enough himself, and helping her would only fan that fire. But instead of turning her down, he'd jumped at the chance to conduct their bonding ritual.

Either Alexander had turned into a hopeless romantic since meeting Catherine, or he felt he owed it to his sister to grant her this request; Lucille wasn't sure which.

Clumsy human footsteps, as well as a rather heady perfume, alerted Lucille to a presence next to her. Speak of the devil; it was Catherine.

"It's beautiful here. I'm jealous," Catherine said.

Lucille turned to face her, though she tried her best not to breathe in too deeply around the woman. The unique quality of her blood still got to her, even though she had recently fed. She thought of something to say, something courteous. *What would Valentino do?*

"You and Alexander can always visit," Lucille said.

"Thank you. I appreciate the offer." Catherine smiled at Lucille, who nodded.

She'd never been good at these shallow niceties. Never felt like she had much time for them.

No, it was something else that danced on the tip of her tongue. Something much deeper and more meaningful.

"Was it worth it?" Lucille asked finally.

Catherine frowned. "What do you mean?"

Lucille nodded at Alexander. "You know. Becoming a vampire's consort?"

Catherine chuckled. "Oh, considering the circumstances… If I hadn't, I might have died that night Julius came to the house to claim me for himself."

Lucille nodded. That was an excellent point.

"Still. It's a lot to give up, isn't it?" Lucille said. "Your old life, your friends and family. The chance for a normal relationship with someone who can leave the house at daytime." *The constant threat of death if one of Alexander's acquaintances lost their control and tried to drain Catherine.* Lucille thought it wise to keep that last remark to herself.

"Honestly, I disagree. He's shown me things I never thought possible. Even if we hadn't been under threat, and I had to do it all over again, I would still marry Alexander."

Lucille watched Valentino, who was still in conversation with Alexander. He'd chosen to spend his life with her. Like Catherine had chosen Alexander.

"Thank you," Lucille mumbled, her voice so low Catherine probably never even heard it. She'd known exactly what Lucille had wanted to hear, though. It had helped put her mind at ease.

They were both only starting on these journeys with their significant others, though. Lucille could only hope that as time passed, Valentino wouldn't change his mind and yearn for his old life back.

He turned away from Alexander and smiled at her, and

she felt reassured. No, he wouldn't want things to go back to the way they were. Not as long as he looked at her like this.

She nodded and left the tiny little wedding party again to retrieve more dishes from inside the house.

When everything was set up, she called out to everyone. "Dinner is served!"

Valentino stepped up to her first, took her hand, and kissed it.

"You didn't need to," he whispered.

"I wanted to," she said.

"You continue to surprise me, Lucille Amboise," Valentino said.

Lucille smiled. It had taken a long time for her to get to this point. Of recognizing a chance at happiness and taking it. Thanks to Valentino, she had found what she'd been missing for hundreds of years.

Love.

They watched as their guests helped themselves to the food on offer.

Tonight was a special night, a unique night. A meal shared with select few to celebrate their union.

But this life of entertaining guests in their lavish home wouldn't be their future. In fact, they probably wouldn't spend much time living here in this old house. She might have left her job with the Council behind, but that hadn't changed Lucille's outlook in life.

The world was much bigger than London. And there

were still creatures—vampires—out there who broke the rules and killed indiscriminately.

Lucille had worried about losing her identity if she left her job with the Council. But together, she and Valentino had come to a compromise. They were not so different from one another; even before they met, they'd done essentially the same thing: brought criminals to justice.

That wasn't just a job; it was a calling. The only difference was, now they no longer had to do it alone.

***

ABOUT THE AUTHOR

Dear Reader,

Thanks for reading Lucille's Valentine. Although at the time I'm writing this it's only been a year and a half since I released my debut series, the Scottish Werebears, I'm not new to writing in general. In fact, my mom still tells me to this day about how I would make up stories, and attempt to record them in my clumsy, shaky handwriting from the moment I learned to read and write. From there I went on to write fan fiction and other stuff meant for my own eyes only.

I've always enjoyed stories of the paranormal. Vampires, shape shifters, witches and magic, all featured in the books I loved the most, even when I was still growing up. But it wasn't until much later that I got into romance. One of the first writers (a self published author just like me!) I came across was Tina Folsom, via her Scanguards Vampire series. I was hooked. From there I went on to read more paranormal romance until I found a new kind of hero I loved: bear shifters, like the kind written by Milly Taiden, Zoe Chant, and T.S. Joyce. What I love about bears is how they can be all strong and independent, a bit reclusive, and almost grumpy, but they always end up having a heart of gold (plus they tend to know their food, and we all know that a man who can cook is doubly sexy). All that (except for the shifting into a powerful bear) almost exactly describes the sort of man I ended up falling for and marrying in real life, so it's no surprise that this is what I started my publishing career with.

But no matter how many bear shifter books I've written, I've always longed to write a Vampire romance. Finally, once the Scottish Werebears series was complete, it was time to fulfill this dream with Alexander's Blood Bride (released in October 2016). And because I couldn't just stop at one, I immediately made plans for a follow-up, Michael's Soul Mate which released the month after. Now, a few months later, I've added a third book, about perhaps the most difficult character so far in the series, Lucille. I hope you had as much fun reading it as I had writing it! By the way, if you'd like to read more about the Vampires of London, do let me know...

To find out more, check:

LoreleiMoone.com (And why not sign up for the newsletter to be the first to find out about new releases.)

You can also get in touch with me via Facebook (search for Lorelei Moone), or email at info@loreleimoone.com

x Lorelei

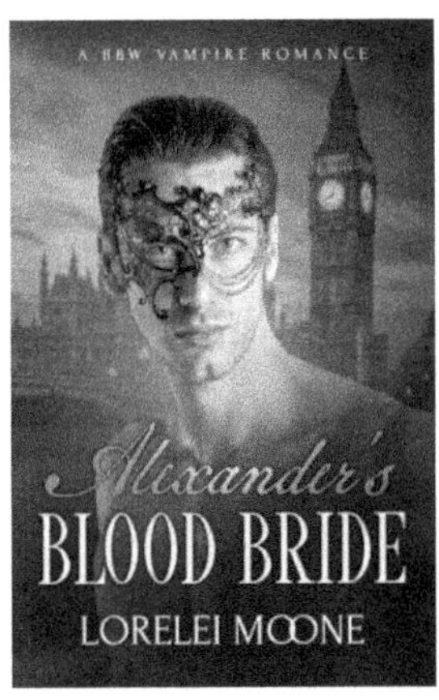

Lucille's Valentine is the third book in the Vampires of London series. Although all books in this series are standalone and can be read out of order, perhaps you'd like to check out the story with which the series started…

About Alexander's Blood Bride

Cat has never been a social butterfly. The only reason she even agreed to go to the stupid Halloween party was because her friend and roommate Shelly wanted to attend. When she gets spooked upon almost falling into bed with the host, she's convinced it was all a big mistake. And what's worse, now people are stalking her wherever she goes!

Alexander Broderick has been hosting his annual Halloween parties for over a century. While his contemporaries use them as an excuse to engage in all kinds of debauchery, his own motives are more benign. He wants to converse, to get a feel for the times they live in through its people. But when Cat walks into his house, he forgets himself and is compelled to seduce her. There's only one problem: she's a so-called Blood Bride – a mortal woman whose blood smells so delicious that every vampire in town wants to drain her.

He knows he's the only one wanting to keep her safe, but can't act as long as she wants nothing to do with him. And then there's his own growing hunger to contend with. Can he protect her from the rest of the vampire community, as well as his own lethal cravings?

It's the ultimate forbidden romance; the love between a mortal and a vampire. What is it that makes flirting with death so utterly tempting? Read on and find out.

Buy a copy on Amazon (ISBN 9781913930288), or get more information on Lorelei Moone's website at loreleimoone.com.

SCOTTISH WEREBEARS

Did you know that Lorelei Moone started her career as an independent author with a whole series dedicated to bear shifters?

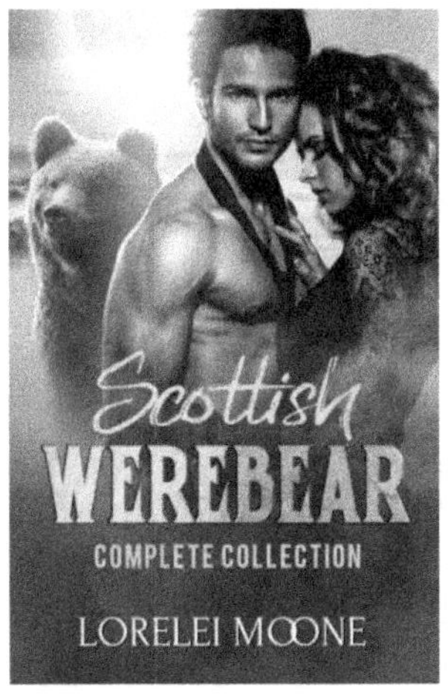

Check out the Scottish Werebears series, now available on all retailers. Book 1, Scottish Werebear: An Unexpected Affair can be downloaded for free in ebook format. All books are also available in paperback as well as audio.

About Scottish Werebear: An Unexpected Affair

Romance novelist, Clarice Adler, has lost the inspiration to write ever since dumping her cheating boyfriend. How do you dream up a plot of two people falling in love, when you've stopped believing in love yourself? But her deadline is looming, and her career hangs in the balance, so she decides to lock herself away on the secluded Scottish Isle of Skye to finish her manuscript. Upon meeting Derek McMillan there, it seems she's found her new muse and the words start to flow out of her as if by magic. Clarice falls for him, hard, despite knowing nothing about the man, except that he's unavailable.

Derek McMillan has been managing his farm and renting out a few holiday cottages on his own for years now. He deals with the occasional tourist for some extra money, but mostly keeps to himself. When he first lays eyes on the curvy beauty, Clarice, he immediately regrets accepting her booking. Lightning strikes, and as much as he tries to deny it, his inner bear knows that she's his mate. But he's a shifter, and she's a human, and the two can't ever mix, can they?

In this steamy paranormal romance novella, follow along as an impossible love blossoms between two people, who couldn't be more different. One might say fate intended for them to meet, if you believe in that sort of thing, but they're both set on fighting their attraction with everything they've got. They're going to need another push to admit to themselves as well as each other what's going on…

Please note that this is the first title in the Scottish Werebears Series. Each book features a different couple from first meeting to HEA, as well as an overarching external plot that won't be fully resolved until the end of the series.

Download your free copy of Scottish Werebear: An Unexpected Affair from your favorite ebook retailer, or get more information on Lorelei Moone's website at loreleimoone.com.